# THE FRAUDULENT GOVERNESS

## Victorian Romance

## FAYE GODWIN

Tica House
Publishing

Sweet Romance that Delights and Enchants!

# PERSONAL WORD FROM THE AUTHOR

**DEAREST READERS,**

I'm so delighted that you have chosen one of my books to read. I am proud to be a part of the team of writers at Tica House Publishing. Our goal is to inspire, entertain, and give you many hours of reading pleasure. Your kind words and loving readership are deeply appreciated.

I would like to personally invite you to sign up for updates and to become part of our **Exclusive Reader Club**—it's completely Free to Join! I'd love to welcome you!

**Much love,**

**Faye Godwin**

## CLICK HERE to Join our Reader's Club and to Receive Tica House Updates!

https://victorian.subscribemenow.com/

# CONTENTS

# PROLOGUE

SOPHIA MORGAN'S scream echoed around the lavish furnishings of her room, a hoarse, animal sound of pain and desperation. Her body tensed in a long, trembling contraction, the bulge of her belly tightening, misshapen under the front of her wrapper. The lower part of the wrapper was unbuttoned, her bare knees jutting shockingly from among the mess of fabric. Elsie Carter had never seen so much of Sophia's skin before. She doubted anyone had, except for Master Simon, but Master Simon was all the way in India now, and he had no idea his first child was coming into the world in the middle of a blizzard.

Sophia's scream and contraction eased at the same time, and she fell back against her sumptuous silk pillows, her sweat-soaked black hair fanning out around her. Her usually porcelain-perfect complexion was blotched with red, and her eyes were desperate as she stared up at Elsie.

"He's coming. He's coming," she panted. "I can't keep him inside."

"Don't try," said Elsie. "Everything is going to be all right." She tried to keep the tremor out of her own voice as she said it.

"All right?" Sophia sobbed with angry sarcasm. "How can it be all right? The snow is three feet deep. There's no calling a midwife, there's no calling a doctor, my mother is long dead, my mother-in-law is frail..." She led out a moan, her head tossing on the pillow. "I'm delivering my baby all alone."

Sophia's hands were lying in bunched fists on the bed on either side of her, and on an impulse, Elsie reached out and wrapped her fingers around one of them. She knew that it was unthinkable for a mere lady's maid to touch her mistress in such a manner, but she also knew Sophia was terrified, and she empathized powerfully with that terror.

"You're not alone, ma'am," she said.

Sophia gave her a desperate look. "What do you know about delivering babies?" She panted, her body shaking as another contraction came for her.

"I delivered my own just a few weeks ago, remember?" said Elsie, managing a smile. Unlike Sophia, she *had* been truly alone, and it had been the most terrifying experience of her life. But she had survived. And so would Sophia, she prayed.

There was no time for further speculation. Sophia let out another shriek of agony, and the piercing sound woke Elsie's baby where she lay wrapped in blankets on the sofa where Elsie had hastily put her down when she'd seen Sophia's sodden bedclothes and known that the baby was coming. Elsie was forced to ignore little Ada's cries as she reached for the young life that was coming into the world, the tiny face squeezing out into the cold air.

"Push, Sophia," she shouted. "The baby's almost here. Push. *Push.*"

Sophia's wail of pain faded, and she fell back again, sobbing and gasping. "I can't," she moaned. "I can't."

The baby's shoulders were still inside. Elsie steadied the tiny head, the motionless little face, and saw how blue the little nose and lips were, and she knew that the baby was in trouble. She lifted her head, her hands shaking on the wet little form as she stared at the frightened girl. Sophia was no older than she was, and she understood that fear, but she also knew what lay beyond it.

"Sophia, I'm trying to ease the baby out, and I can't," she said. "Listen to me."

Sophia's eyes fluttered open, perhaps in shock that Elsie would dare to address her by her first name.

"Your baby needs you now," said Elsie. "It needs you to push, or it's not going to survive. You need to save your baby, right *now*. Do you understand?"

Sophia stared at her for a few moments, her terror obvious. Then something flickered in her eyes, something furious and fearless that Elsie knew all too well, for just a few weeks ago she'd felt it in her own chest. It seemed to her then that perhaps, despite the fact that Elsie lived down in the cold and dark servants' quarters and Sophia lived in these sumptuous surroundings, they were not all that different after all.

"All right." Sophia gritted her teeth, and when the next contraction came, her sound was no scream of agony. It was a roar of fury, the sound of a woman who had found herself in an instant transformed into a mother, a sound of rage. Suddenly the baby was slipping abruptly toward Elsie, and the next minute it was in her arms, wet and wriggling and gloriously alive, its tiny cries echoing through the room, matching Ada's little voice, the wonderful sound of new life.

"It's a boy." Elsie gasped, delighted, as she grabbed for a clean towel and swaddled the baby in it. "It's a little boy."

Sophia was struggling to sit up, tears and sweat gleaming on her cheeks. "Give him to me," she croaked, her arms held out. "Give him to me."

Elsie wasted no time in dealing with the umbilical cord and then setting the baby in his mother's arms. Sophia clutched him close, cuddling him up against her face despite the blood and fluid that smeared her cheek. She was crying as she hung onto him, her sweaty hair hanging around her face. Slowly, the baby's cries quieted somewhat, and he blinked up at her with the brightest blue eyes that Elsie had ever seen on a baby. They were as bright as little Ada's eyes were dark.

"He's beautiful," she breathed.

"He's perfect." Sophia gave a rippling little laugh, looking up at Elsie. "Oh, Elsie, he's just perfect." Her smile was utterly radiant, her eyes alight, and she turned them back on her baby, touching the tip of his tiny nose, tracing a finger down the curve of his chubby little cheek.

"Let me wash him for you, Sophia," said Elsie softly. "I've heated some water."

"Just let me hold him for a moment longer." Sophia's arms tightened around the baby. "Just a moment longer."

"Of course." Elsie was relieved to hurry to her own baby, scooping tiny Ada up into her arms. The child quietened immediately, looking up at Elsie with her black eyes, calmness coming over her. Silence fell in the room except for Sophia's gentle cooing. Elsie rocked Ada in her arms, slowly getting the baby back to sleep.

She turned to Sophia as Ada's eyes closed. "Do you have a name for him?" she asked softly.

Sophia looked up at her, beaming. "Simon and I decided on a name before he left for India," she said. "He'll be named after my own father." She kissed the baby's little forehead. "Quincy. Quincy Morgan."

"It's a beautiful name," said Elsie.

"He's a beautiful baby," said Sophia.

Elsie came a little closer to gaze down at the baby boy, almost as captivated by the new little life as Sophia was. Her mistress looked up at her, then reached out a trembling hand, laying it on Elsie's arm.

"Thank you," Sophia whispered. "I could never have done this without you, Elsie." She squeezed her arm. "Please – what can I do for you? How can I help you?"

Elsie shook her head, even though it was tempting to answer with a long list of wants. "No, ma'am. I couldn't ask anything of you. I'm just happy your little one is all right."

"Well, then I'll make a promise on my own." Sophia clutched her arm, her eyes and voice fervent. "You saved my little Quincy's life, and I'm forever in your debt. So you must know that I will always care for you, Elsie, and for your little baby. You and Ada will never want for anything for as long as I live."

It would be easy to dismiss those words as the rapturous ramblings of an excited new mother, but when Elsie looked into Sophia's eyes, she saw that fierce determination in them again.

"And I'll serve you and little Quincy with all my heart, Sophia," said Elsie, "for as long as I live."

And so their friendship was formed, in blood and snow, a friendship that would change everything.

# PART I

# CHAPTER 1

*Eleven Years Later*

ADA'S GIGGLES were captive in her chest, trapped there like bubbles. She kept one hand over her mouth, determined not to let them out, and tucked herself a little deeper behind the curtain. Quincy would never think to look for her here. She was tucked snugly into the gap beside the bust of Quincy's great-grandfather, the drapes of the big hall window hiding her from sight. Now if only she could stay perfectly quiet, he would never find her. She would finally make him give up.

She heard his footsteps coming up the hall and muffled her giggles all the more. He had no reason to stifle his own, though; she could hear his musical laughter as he checked all her usual hiding spots, the doorways and statues, the shadows behind the suit of armour some bygone ancestor had worn in some forgotten war.

His footsteps came closer. Ada tucked herself a little deeper into her niche, holding her breath. She saw the drapes stir as he reached for them, then muttered to himself, "No... no. She won't go in there, not with the spiders."

It was all Ada could do to restrain herself from a yell of triumph. What Quincy didn't know was that Ada had convinced Mama to remove the spiders.

His footsteps pattered away back toward the nursery, and Ada let out her breath in a whoosh. Several more minutes ticked by; it was boring behind the drapes, but Ada was more than content to do a little waiting before her great victory. Finally, when the big clock in the downstairs hall tolled out the quarter, Quincy's voice rang in the hall.

"All right. All right," he shouted. "You win. I can't find you."

He sounded wonderfully close to her, and so it was all too easy to throw back the drapes and leap out of her nook with a terrifying roar. Quincy let out a satisfyingly high-pitched squeal, spinning around and throwing up his hands, and Ada almost fainted with laughter. Hands on her belly, she tipped back her head and laughed and laughed and laughed.

"That's not funny, Ada," Quincy squeaked.

"You scream like a girl," Ada chortled. "Just like a girl."

"I do not." Quincy stomped one shiny shoe.

"Yes, you do."

For a moment, a flash of irritation crossed Quincy's face, and Ada thought he might be about to fly into one of his silly little tempers. Instead, he relaxed into a grin.

"Well, all right, then." He gave her a playful little mock punch in the arm. "You've finally beaten me. It only took you eleven years."

"Ha. I'll beat you for another eleven years, too," said Ada.

"What's all this mafficking?" demanded a nasal voice, and the housemaid came striding along the corridor, carrying a bucket and mop. She gave Ada a vicious look. "Don't you have work to do, child?"

"I did all my chores, Peggy," said Ada. "Mama said we could play."

"Your mama isn't the housekeeper around here, much as she acts like it," snapped Peggy.

"Don't talk to Ada like that." Quincy planted his hands on his hips. "If you're unhappy with her, then talk to my mama about it."

Peggy glared at him, and Ada knew Quincy had played his trump card. Sweet Sophia would never speak against Ada, and especially not against Mama.

"Children should be seen and not heard," said Peggy. "Haven't you ever been told that?"

She swept down the hall, and Ada sighed, watching her go. "I don't understand, Quincy," she said. "No one likes me or Mama at all, except for you and your mother. Not even your father likes seeing you and me play together." She frowned. "I don't understand why."

"It's because you're a maid's daughter, and I'm a gentleman's son. That's what Mama said when I asked her about it," said Quincy. "But it's all rot if you ask me, anyway. Why should there be any difference? We can still be friends."

"I'm glad your papa didn't send you to boarding school," said Ada.

"Me too, even if it means that he keeps going on and on about me taking over his business and learning about the trade and all that sort of thing," said Quincy. "I hardly understand a word of it in any case. But at least I get to stay at home and play with you." He grinned, his eyes sparkling with mischief, and then he lunged to slap a hand lightly on her back. "You're It!"

He bolted, and Ada ran after him, their laughter filling the hallways of Morgan House. And even though Quincy was the only person her age that Ada knew, she was certain, then, that Quincy was more than enough.

MR. WOLSELY SEEMED to be mostly blind, squinting down at his book through his thick half-moon glasses, but that had never stopped him from shooting angry glances in Ada's direction even though she was sitting very quietly in the corner of the nursery. She froze, knowing that her slate pencil had scraped a little too loudly, and he glared at her for a few long moments.

"You were saying, Mr. Wolsely?" said Quincy primly, with a little edge to his voice.

Mr. Wolsely let out a deep sigh of annoyance and went back to a droning lesson about multiplication. He was reading out equations from a book, and Ada had to move quickly to write them down on her slate. At least numbers were easier than letters; Ada found ciphering far easier than reading, even though Quincy always complained about how difficult it was.

Having read out the work, Mr. Wolsely excused himself briefly to go to the washroom, and the children bowed their heads over their slates. Ada started to scribble down her answers, her tongue sticking out in concentration.

"Psst." Quincy twisted in his chair, looking over her shoulder at her. "What's the answer to number three?"

"I'm not going to tell you," Ada retorted, giggling. "Work it out yourself."

"Ugh. These numbers make my head spin." Quincy sighed. "You know, when Mama told Mr. Wolsely that you were to sit in on my lessons, I was hoping that you would at least help me with some answers."

"How could I?" Ada giggled, deepening her voice to mimic Mr. Wolsely. "*A girl child? Learning mathematics? Preposterous. And a low-class little waif like this, too.*"

They both chuckled but fell immediately silent and bowed their heads when the door banged open. But it wasn't Mr. Wolsely. It was Mama.

"Ada, my pet, you need to come with me," she said quickly, her face a little pale as she held out a hand to her.

"Why, Mama?" Ada felt a jolt of fear. "What's the matter?"

"Nothing at all, my love." Mama managed a wobbly smile. "Master Ralph has just arrived for a visit, that's all."

"Hooray!" Quincy jumped out of his chair. "I love playing with Uncle Ralph."

"I want to play with him, too, Mama," said Ada.

Mama's face grew even paler, a strange look flashing across it. "No. You can't," she said sharply. "Now stop talking back to me and come with me at once."

Ada withdrew, startled by Mama's tone. Mama never spoke to her like that. It sounded like she'd done something wrong, and that frightened her. "Why are you angry with me?"

"I'm not angry with you, Ada." Mama sighed. "But you have to come with me, right now. Do you understand?"

Ada was a little comforted by the love in her mother's tone. She reached out and took her hand, and Mama pulled her off her feet.

"But what about our ciphering, Elsie?" Quincy called after them.

"It'll have to wait. Now you play with your uncle and don't worry about Ada, there's a good boy," Mama said, her voice trembling.

Mama was leading her down the stairs, then along the narrow hallway to the kitchen. Through the kitchen, she took the hall that led to the servants' quarters, where they had a cozy room. Ada liked their room, but it would be so boring at this time of day. She'd already read all the old books that Sophia had given her.

"Do I have to go to bed now, Mama?" she asked.

"No, my love. You just need to stay in our room for a few days," said Mama.

"A few days." Ada sighed. "Why do I always have to hide when Master Ralph is here?"

"I'll tell you one day, when you're older."

"But I *am* older." Ada felt a pang of annoyance. She just wanted to get back to her studies and to playing with Quincy.

It was already bad enough that she had to pretend not to be friends with Quincy whenever his father was home; she hated that she had to hide every time his uncle came over.

"Well, not old enough," said Mama brusquely.

Ada was startled to see Sophia waiting at the entrance to their room. She was holding a few old, well-thumbed books, and she gave Ada a sad little smile.

"Here, sweetie," she said, holding out the books. "I think you've read these already, but the governess was cleaning out Quincy's room and needed space for some new books, so I wanted to give you these."

Ada smiled up at Quincy's sweet, gentle mother. "Thank you," she said.

"Go inside now, there's a good girl," said Sophia.

Ada clutched the books to her chest as she went into the room, and Elsie closed the door behind her with a quiet click. Setting the books down on the bed she shared with Elsie, Ada sat on the edge of the bed beside them, staring out of the single little window. It was a foggy, rainy morning, and she couldn't even see all the way to the end of the garden. She wished she could.

There were soft voices outside the door, and Ada felt the urge to put her ear to the keyhole and hear what Sophia and Mama were talking about. She hesitated. Mama had always told her that eavesdropping was a wicked thing to do, but she just couldn't understand why no one would tell her the reason for hiding her away when Master Ralph came over. Quincy always had the most wonderful stories to tell after one of his uncle's visits, about going fishing or playing games in the living room and about how his uncle was clever and kind and funny and wonderful. Ada couldn't understand why she was hidden away from him all the time.

She stepped off the bed and tiptoed over to the door, crouching down to place her ear against the keyhole.

"... tell her the truth," Elsie was saying.

"You can't, Elsie," said Sophia. "How would the poor child feel if she found out? She's far too young to understand such things."

Ada pressed her ear a little more tightly against the keyhole. What were they talking about?

Elsie sighed. "You're right. And what good would it do, in any case?"

"None at all. Tell her when she's older – much older – and can understand." Sophia sighed. "Besides, if you tell her, she'll tell Quincy, and he'll never look at his uncle in the same light again."

"Perhaps he shouldn't." There was an edge to Mama's voice. "I know you don't."

"How could I, after what he did?" Sophia said. "But Quincy is enjoying a wonderful childhood, and part of that is due to Ralph and how he spoils him. I don't want to take that away from him without a very good reason."

They were moving down the hallway now, and their voices disappeared into the kitchen before Ada could hear any more. She straightened up, feeling more confused than ever. What had Master Ralph done that she couldn't understand? And why would it make even Sophia, his own sister-in-law, doubt him? It had always seemed to Ada that they must have good a relationship, considering that his wife − Quincy's father's sister − had died a few years ago, but he still came to visit Quincy's parents even though they were no blood relatives of his.

It was another mystery in a world full of grown-up mysteries. Ada cast herself on the bed with a sigh and picked up a book. At least she could rest and read a little, she supposed.

But she'd rather be playing with Quincy. And she'd rather know the truth.

# CHAPTER 2

MASTER RALPH'S visit lasted for three long, boring days. Ada wasn't allowed outside at all. She had to stay in her room, or in the kitchen, or in the tiny communal bathroom that all the servants shared. She didn't mind any of those rooms – they were clean and nice – but no one seemed to want to talk to her, not even the little scullery-maid, who was about her own age.

She was trying to make friends with her on the third evening. The scullery-maid was a mousy little slip of a child with big black eyes, the daughter of one of the housemaids, and right this minute she was standing at the kitchen sink, scrubbing away at the dishes. Ada usually did the breakfast dishes before tutoring sessions, when Macy was busy with washing the floors. She approached her slowly, almost worried that she might scare her off like a frightened mouse.

"I'll rinse and dry for you, if you like," she said.

Macy turned her dark eyes on Ada. "Why?" she demanded. "You never usually help with the dinner dishes."

Ada stepped back, a little shocked. "Mama says I don't have to," she said.

"Of course, she does. And I'm sure Mistress Sophia doesn't mind one bit."

"Mistress Sophia is the one who said I should only do the breakfast dishes," said Ada, prickled. "She wants me to get on with my studies."

"Your studies." Macy let out an angry little snort, slamming a stack of plates into the soapy water. "Don't make me laugh."

"I'm not joking." Ada frowned at her, puzzled. "I... I don't understand why you're angry with me."

"Well, you should," said Macy. "Don't I deserve a chance to learn things, too, and to play, and to have friends like you do?"

Ada said nothing. She suddenly didn't want Macy to know she didn't really have any friends other than Quincy.

Macy turned back to the dishes, splashing angrily around in the soapy water. Ada took a hesitant step forward. "Maybe you can finish your work a bit earlier, if I help you with those dishes now," she said.

"The cook won't let me." Macy's voice was sad and defeated now. "Just leave me alone, Ada."

Ada backed away, fighting the tears that stung her eyes. She was about to turn and go back to their room when there was a deafening thundering along the hallway to the kitchen. The next moment, Quincy came charging into the scullery, wearing a pirate hat and carrying two wooden swords.

"Ahoy, matey." he cackled, tossing one of the swords to Ada. "Uncle Ralph has gone home and look what he brought me."

"Swords," cried Ada, brandishing hers. "Just what you wanted."

"What on Earth is this?" thundered the cook's voice. She loomed in the doorway of the scullery, her many chins wobbling with furious rage. "Children in my kitchen? How dare you come in here." She seized a broom. "Get out of my kitchen."

Quincy let out a chuckle. "Governess won't be happy, either." he said. "Run, Ada."

They bolted, ducking under the cook's arms and out of the kitchen. Shrieking with laughter, Ada fell into step easily with Quincy as they bounded up the stairs to the nursery. They paused on the second-floor landing for a brief but spirited swordfight, and that was when Mama came around the corner, carrying a bundle of dirty laundry.

"Ada," she cried out, shocked. "That is *not* how a young lady conducts herself."

"She's no lady," said Quincy. "She's a maid, so she can do what she pleases."

"She most certainly cannot, young man," said Mama severely. "Put that toy away at once, Ada. I don't mind you playing with Quincy, but you'll play like a little girl, not a boy."

Ada knew better than to contradict Mama when she used that tone. She lowered the sword demurely, giving it to Quincy. "Yes, Mama."

Mama bustled off, and Quincy turned to Ada. "I'm sorry," he said. "I didn't want to get you into trouble. I just wanted to try out my swords, and Uncle Ralph said I should play with my friends, but I don't really have any friends other than you."

"I know," said Ada.

"I'm glad I have you, though." Quincy's voice was sincere, his big blue eyes very wide. "With all the studying Papa makes me do, and the time he spends taking me to his offices and things and wanting me to learn about them and all that, I wouldn't have time to play with friends even if I had them."

"You do have me, though." Ada giggled. "So don't be so serious. Let's play some hide-and-seek, instead."

"All right." Quincy sighed, putting down his swords and pirate hat. "Don't you think it's a bit silly?"

"What is?" asked Ada.

"That boys can do some things, and girls, other things. Why, you'll be just as good a swordfighter as any boy, I think."

Ada smiled. "And do you think you'd be just as good a cook?"

"Maybe," said Quincy boldly.

Ada burst into fits of laughter at the thought. "You're the silly one, Quincy," she said. "Especially since you think you can beat me again at hide-and-seek."

A slow grin spread over his features. "Oh, I don't *think*," he said. "I *know*."

"Prove it," said Ada.

He laughed. "All right."

She covered her eyes and began to count out loud, and she heard the ripple of Quincy's laughter and the patter of his footsteps as he ran off to hide. But she knew that it wouldn't take her long to find him.

She always found Quincy again, in the end.

⌘

ADA COULD SEE that Quincy was unhappy. He squirmed in his seat, staring down at the slate in front of him. On the other side of the desk, his father, Master Simon, leaned forward with his elbows resting on the desk. His eyes were fixed firmly on his son, and there was something cold and unyielding in his expression that had always frightened Ada.

She looked away quickly, focusing on the ornaments she was dusting along the mantelpiece. When she'd volunteered to dust the nursery, she'd been hoping that Quincy would be alone so they could play a little or even just talk. It always annoyed her, on the rare weekends that Master Simon was home all the time, that she could hardly spend any time with Quincy. Instead, even though it was a Sunday afternoon, Master Simon seemed to have cornered Quincy with an arithmetic problem. It was long division, and when Ada had glanced at the slate out of the corner of her eye, she was quite sure the answer he had written there was wrong.

Quincy hated arithmetic, and his face was starting to get increasingly red as he stared down at it.

"Come on now, son," said Master Simon, his voice very stiff and tight. "Check your work."

"I... I have checked it." Quincy raised his head, his eyes a little frightened. "I think it's right, Papa. I really do."

Master Simon sat back in his chair with an angry little huff, and Quincy's shoulders slumped. Ada wished she could disappear. But she didn't want to seem suspicious, so she went on dusting as quickly as she could.

"Quincy, I don't think you understand the gravity of your own education," said Master Simon grimly. "You can't spend all of your time fooling around like this. You need to work hard, as I did, or you'll never get anywhere in life – and Morgan Enterprises will be utterly ruined once it's under your control."

"No, Papa," said Quincy quickly. "I won't ruin it."

"You most certainly will, if you continue to fail to apply yourself to your studies," snapped Master Simon.

"I'm trying, Papa," said Quincy. "We have two arithmetic lessons every day, and I really do try, I really do. Ask Mr. Wolsely."

"Mr. Wolsely is of the opinion that you are an intelligent boy who simply cannot be bothered to spend any effort in your classes," said Master Simon. "This cannot continue."

"Papa, I work hard," said Quincy. "I…"

"That cannot be true. No true Morgan will have such difficulty with arithmetic if they are truly trying."

Ada's toes curled inside her shoes for Quincy. She knew how hard he tried in his lessons, but, of course, she couldn't come to his defense. That much she knew full well, and her mother hardly ever had to warn her that she should always be invisible when Master Simon was around. She'd only ever spoken to him once, to say a cheerful good morning, but the look he had given her had made it abundantly clear that she was not welcome to speak in his presence – or even to exist, except for his own convenience.

He was giving poor Quincy that same look now.

"The whole reason why you have never been sent to boarding school is because you must become an adept businessman, Quincy. Your education must be specialized and exacting. And arithmetic is central to that."

"I know, Papa," said Quincy, "I just…"

"Are you talking back to me?"

Master Simon's words rang down over Quincy's shoulders like a blow. Ada flinched for his part. Quincy looked up at his father, and for a moment it almost seemed as though he would say something. As though he would stand up to Master Simon, as inconceivable as that was.

Instead, the boy's shoulders slumped, and he stared down at the floor.

"No, Papa," he murmured. And even as he spoke, it seemed to Ada that she could see the spirit leaving him.

# CHAPTER 3

"Pssst."

Ada could barely hear the tiny sound over the hiss of the scrubbing brush on the floor of Sophia's bedroom. She looked up, glancing around, but there was no one to be seen; just the rich, shining mahogany of the damp floor, and the big windows with their rippling lace curtains, and Sophia's four-poster bed all draped in its thick covers. She must have imagined it. It would be little surprise if she was imagining things, she thought. She was growing so tired and lonely after Master Simon had been home for three weeks that she felt she might be about to go mad.

Dipping the brush in the bucket, she wearily set back to work on scrubbing the floor.

"Pssst. Ada."

This time, there was no mistaking the sound. Ada looked over her shoulder. Quincy had put his head around the door, and when her eyes found his, he gave a wide, mischievous smile. "Come here," he whispered.

"Quincy." Ada grinned, rising to her feet.

"Hush, hush," Quincy hissed. "Papa's in his study. We don't want him to hear us, or it'll ruin everything. Come on."

Ada hesitantly set down the brush and came over to the doorway. It was so good to speak with Quincy. Of course, she'd seen him all the time since Master Simon came home, but it felt as though they hadn't had a real conversation in weeks.

"Are you sure he's in his study?" she whispered back.

"Yes, it's all right. No one will see you with me." Quincy sighed, rolling his eyes. "It's such a frightful bore that you can't play with me when Papa is here."

"I don't understand it," said Ada.

"It's because you're a maid's daughter, that's why."

"I know that much," said Ada. "I just don't know why it should matter whose daughter I am. Besides, Mama is a lovely person, much nicer than your papa."

"That's true," snorted Quincy. "You won't believe all the extra schoolwork he's been making me do. And he's always so cold, and never any fun. I can't wait until he goes off to Liverpool next week." He shook his head.

"So why can't I play with you, just because my mama is a maid?" Ada ran a hand over her chin. "It just doesn't make sense to me, Quin. Aren't we the same?"

"Of course, we're the same," said Quincy easily. "Papa just doesn't understand that. He thinks he's better than everyone." He put a hand over his mouth, stifling a giggle. "But he'll be humiliated in a moment."

Ada recognized the mischief in Quincy's eyes. "What have you done?"

"Come and see," said Quincy, grabbing her hand. "And be very quiet."

They tiptoed down the hall to Master Simon's study, and Ada could hear him muttering inside it. There was a papery rustle, the thump of books being moved.

"He's writing important letters," said Quincy, with a little scorn in his voice. "Peep through the keyhole."

Ada peered inside. Master Simon was sitting at his desk, scribbling furiously. His fountain pen, however, seemed to be running out of ink. Annoyed, Master Simon reached for the inkwell. Quincy made a small, choked sound, stifling a giggle, as Master Simon filled his pen.

"You didn't," Ada breathed.

"I did," chuckled Quincy.

Master Simon was back to writing again, but as he wrote, his frown deepened, and his pen was moving more and more slowly. After a few moments, he tugged at the pen, and with a small sound a piece of paper ripped off, clinging to the pen.

"Glue in the inkwell," hissed Quincy, his eyes streaming with barely contained mirth.

"We'd better run," whispered Ada.

"QUINCY!" Master Simon's roar of rage echoed through the study.

Quincy and Ada turned and bolted, trying their best to swallow the giggles that were fizzing madly inside them. Ada made it back to the bedroom, grabbed a brush and got back to furiously working while Quincy disappeared outside. She heard the thunder of Master Simon's footsteps pass the doorway in pursuit of Quincy and could only hope he wouldn't be caught.

Master Simon deserved every prank his son could play on him.

❧

IT WAS A PERFECT DAY, warm and summery, the world all painted in blues and greens as the rich sunshine poured down onto the city. Ada longed to go outside and play on the long green lawn, its rich, even sweep easily visible through the kitchen window. Any other summer day she would most certainly have been out there already, playing with Quincy. There were so many wonderful games to play on that lawn: conkers with the chestnuts from the tall trees lining it; tag on the grass; hide-and-seek in the hedge. Sometimes Quincy insisted on playing catch, although Ada preferred hopscotch.

Her mind was filled with happy games, but her hands were plunged into the sink, and she didn't stop scrubbing as she stared out into the gorgeous summer day. Just three more days, she told herself. She only had to wait three more days before Master Simon went off to Liverpool for a week, and her life could finally go back to its happy normal.

She let out a fluttering sigh and turned her attention back to the dishes. Mama came in carrying a pot, cup, and saucer from Sophia's usual mid-morning tea. She put it down on the sideboard and started fussing about by the stove. Her voice sounded ragged, almost frightened, and Ada looked up, a ripple of shock running through her body.

"Mama?" she asked. "What's the matter?"

"Nothing − nothing, sweetheart," said Mama, her voice distant. "Just − bring me that ginger, would you? And the honey."

Ada dried her hands and hurried to the pantry, coming back with a stick of ginger and the honeypot. "Are you sick?" she asked. "You always give me tea with ginger and honey when I'm sick."

"No one is sick," said Mama, but her voice was shaking, and Ada wasn't sure that she was telling the truth. She grasped a grater and started shaving off bits of the ginger. "Bring me a good china teacup."

A nasty jolt ran through Ada's body. "Is it Sophia?"

Mama said nothing, but the way her jaw was clenched told Ada everything that she needed to know. A black pit of fear opened in her stomach, and her thoughts flew to Quincy.

"But Mama, the doctor said that if Sophia fell ill again..."

"I know what the doctor said," Mama snapped. "Now bring me that teacup."

Mama never snapped. Ada realized that her mother must be terrified, and the thought frightened her even more. Two winters ago, Sophia had been deathly ill, so ill that a black pall had hung over the house for weeks. But it had all turned out fine; Sophia had gotten better, and she had taken Quincy, Mama, and Ada to the seaside for the summer, which had been wonderful. Yet the doctor's dire words still hung over her head. Ada had thought they would never come true.

"Is it the flu again, Mama?" Ada asked quietly.

Mama didn't answer the question. "Bring the tray with the teacup and follow me," she ordered, grasping the teapot, and striding off up the stairs.

Her heart in her mouth, Ada followed.

SOPHIA'S ethereal beauty was by no means diminished by the grey pallor of her face. She lay back against her pillows, sweat beading on her forehead, her arms listlessly on top of the covers. Her usually perfect hair was a tangled cloud around her head now, and there was suffering in her bloodshot eyes.

She kept them trained on Mama, though, and not on the doctor standing by her bedside, nor Master Simon where he hovered by the doorway. Mama was sitting on the edge of the bed, gently sponging Sophia's brow with lukewarm water from the bucket that Ada was holding. Ada wanted to stare down into the bucket instead of up at Sophia's face, but somehow, she couldn't look away.

It had only been two days since Sophia had started to feel ill, but Dr. Hobbs had a grim look on his face as he placed his stethoscope on her chest.

"How has the fever been?" he asked Mama.

"Not too bad so far, sir. It broke in the night but came back this morning." Mama's voice was trembling in a way that made Ada feel sick with fear.

"As it does." Dr. Hobbs sighed. "I'll leave you with more medicine. Continue to give her laudanum—it will help her sleep." He put a hand on Sophia's arm. "You'll feel better after that, Mrs. Morgan."

Sophia gave a quaking smile. "Can I see my boy?" she whispered, her voice raw and faded. "Can I see my little Quincy?"

"Not right now. You need to rest," said Dr. Hobbs. "Peace and quiet – that's what you need."

A tear trickled down Sophia's cheek. "I want to see Quincy."

"And you'll see him soon," said Mama soothingly, sponging the side of Sophia's face. "You just need a little sleep first, then I'll bring Quincy in to say hello."

Sophia let out a fluttering sigh. Dr. Hobbs gave Mama a vial of something, and Sophia drank it, then lay back on the pillows and closed her eyes.

"Let her be for now," said Dr. Hobbs.

Mama motioned for Ada to leave the room, and she stepped outside into the hallway. Master Simon was standing there, shifting his weight from foot to foot, grabbing his pocket-watch from time to time and glaring down at its face. At the end of the hall, on the landing, Ada could just see Quincy's frightened face peering up from behind the banisters of the top step.

Master Simon put his watch away when Dr. Hobbs came outside. "Well?" he said impatiently.

"I'm afraid your wife is very ill, Mr. Morgan," said Dr. Hobbs. "The influenza is very dangerous for her on top of her weak chest. She needs to be cared for diligently and around the clock if she is to survive."

Ada didn't think Dr. Hobbs had seen Quincy on the landing. Quincy's eyes grew huge at those words, and tears were pooling in them. If Master Simon hadn't been standing there, Ada would have run to him.

Master Simon nodded curtly. "Well, Elspeth, that's what you're here for," he said.

Mama's hands tightened on the sponge, wringing it out like she would want to be wringing Master Simon's neck instead. "I won't leave her side, sir," she said stiffly.

"Miss Carter has done an admirable job so far," said Dr. Hobbs. "I will return daily, and you are to send me a note if there is any sudden worsening. I will leave you a honey balsam for her chest."

"Are you doing all that can be done, doctor?" asked Master Simon.

"Yes, sir."

"Very well, then." Master Simon turned away, shooting Mama a cold look. "Continue to care for my wife in my absence."

"Absence?" cried Mama. "Sir, surely you're not still going to Liverpool?"

"Of course, I am. My business is there." Master Simon turned away. "See to it that Sophia is well upon on my return."

"Sir..." Mama began, but Master Simon was already heading down the stairs. To his mind, the whole matter had been dismissed.

# CHAPTER 4

ADA'S NECK ached when she woke two mornings later. She lay very still, listening to the sound of deep, rattling breathing, and the trickle of water into the bucket as Mama wrung out her cloth. That sound had become the background to their days now; Ada hadn't slept in her own bed for a long time. She lay curled up on the hearth rug instead with a pillow under her head and an old rug over her. She felt as though she had mostly been forgotten.

Thirsty and hungry, she sat up, rubbing the back of her neck. "Mama?" she whispered.

"Ada, darling, can you run and bring me some more hot water?" Mama asked.

She was almost as pale as Sophia. Her voice was a distant wisp of a thing, as insubstantial as mist blown away by a cold wind. Her eyes were dull, staring, exhausted. Sophia's cheeks were hollows of grey, and her chest heaved with every struggling breath, her closed eyes bright red against her white face.

Ada stood up slowly. "I'm hungry, Mama."

"Ask the housekeeper to get you something later," said Mama irritably. "Please bring me that water right away." She indicated the jug by her feet.

Ada stretched, her sore neck sending pangs into her shoulders. She came over to Mama, laying a hand on her arm. "I don't think she'll give me anything," she said in a small voice.

"Oh, Ada." Mama tugged her arm away. "Don't fuss so. Can't you see that Sophia needs me?"

Ada wanted to get angry, but Mama's voice cracked on the last syllable. A tear trickled down her cheek, and Ada felt a surge of breath-taking fear. Mama was never cruel to her like this. Why was everything changing so quickly? What had she done wrong?

She picked up the jug and stumbled toward the kitchen, feeling as though she was living in a bad dream. Her feet were silent in their stockings as she moved down the hallway, her damp hair tickling her shoulders. Everything had been so wonderful. But now things had gone so wrong. And what if Sophia died?

Her hands wobbled on the pitcher, and she stopped on the landing, taking deep breaths in an effort to swallow her tears. What then?

There was a quiet, sobbing noise to her left, and she swallowed her own tears, startled. Whipping around, she saw that it was Quincy. He was sitting in a huddled heap by the banisters, his hair unbrushed, his face dirty, clothes rumpled. His eyes were very red, and his nose was running.

Ada lowered the jug. "Quin?"

He dragged a sleeve over his nose and turned his face away. "Go away, Ada," he mumbled.

It was a very half-hearted mumble. Ada set down the jug and sat on the step beside him, sliding a little closer. Quincy squeezed himself against the banisters as though he wanted to disappear.

She almost asked him what was the matter, but of course, she already knew. So she just sat beside him in silence for a few long moments, wondering what to say.

Before she could think of something, Quincy spoke first. "Is my mama going to die?" he asked quietly.

The words drove a pang of icy fear down into the pit of Ada's belly. She swallowed it. Sophia dying was unimaginable. It would change everything... and for Quincy, it would be far worse. She tried to imagine losing her own mother, but her mind flinched back, refusing to go to that unspeakable place.

He was still waiting for an answer. Ada wished she knew what to say, but she didn't, and his face was crumpling like a crushed paper rose, wobbling with effort as he fought to keep from crying. She felt sorry for him then. No one should have to hold back their tears at a time like this. So she went over to him and put an arm around his shoulders, awkwardly, because he was already a little taller than she was.

Even then, she didn't know what to say. But when Quincy pressed his face into her shoulder, she felt that maybe there was nothing to say at all.

❧

*TICK, tock. Tick, tock.*

The sonorous rhythm of the grandfather clock in the hall was the only sound in the house, save for the gentle thumps from upstairs – the sound of the doctors moving around in Sophia's bedroom. Where Ada and Quincy sat side by side on the stairs, neither of them could make out any of the words, just hushed, hurried voices.

*Tick, tock. Tick, tock.*

Ada was starving. Mama hadn't come out of Sophia's room at all in the past two days, and for those days, she'd slept curled on the kitchen hearth rug, ignored by all of the other servants. She'd asked Cookie for something to eat a few times, but Cookie always told her that she was much too busy, even though Ada had definitely heard Mama asking Cookie to take care of her while she was nursing Sophia. That was the last time Ada had seen her mother: in the kitchen two afternoons ago, her face as drawn and haggard as that of her patient. That was soon before the second doctor had been called in.

*Tick, tock. Tick, tock.*

Quincy's face was strangely pale and frozen. Even his eyes seemed washed-out and distant, as though all of the crying had diluted their vibrant colour. He said nothing, but Ada could feel him shaking slightly where his shoulder pressed against her own as they sat together like a vigil.

*Tick, tock. Tick, tock.*

Ada couldn't remember a time that the house had been so silent. Especially not when she and Quincy were together. There was always talking, laughter. If no one else, at least Mama and Sophia would be chattering all day. With their voices both silent, it was as though the very heart of the house had stopped beating. A terrible hush had fallen over the entire house; even the gossiping kitchen maids were terse and tight-lipped in the face of the danger that might await them all.

*Tick, tock. Tick, tock.*

With the brisk clopping of serious shoes on the polished floor, Miss Hardwick, Quincy's governess, strode into the room and shot a disapproving look up the stairs.

"There you are, young Mr. Morgan," she said angrily, her voice cutting painfully through the silence, which had felt as sacred as it was exhausting. "I thought you were practicing your reading in the nursery like a good boy while I went down for your lunch."

"I'm not hungry," mumbled Quincy, dropping his eyes to the ground. "And I don't feel like reading."

"Well, you shall both eat and read, or you'll be sorry." barked Miss Hardwick. "Now come with me for your lunch at once."

Quincy rose reluctantly to his feet, and Ada rose with him. Any formality or propriety had fled her in the face of her rising hunger. "Please, Miss Hardwick," she said, "may I come along with Quincy to lunch? I'm ever so hungry."

She felt sure that Miss Hardwick would take her to the nursery at once. After all, when Master Simon wasn't around, Sophia often let her have Quincy's leftovers. But now, Miss Hardwick recoiled as though Ada had suggested she pick up a live viper.

"What?" she cried. "Eat with the young master? You're out of your mind, you stupid little maid." She grabbed Quincy by the arm, wrenching him to his feet.

"I don't want to go," Quincy squirmed. "I want to stay here, nearer Mama."

"Well, you're coming with me," barked Miss Hardwick, "and you're going down to the kitchens where you belong, maid."

"She's not just a maid," snapped Quincy. "She's my friend. You have to give her something to eat." He pulled his arm free and took a step back from her, clutching it to his chest as though her grip had hurt him.

Miss Hardwick gave Ada a look of old, festering hatred that took her breath away with its force. Before she could say anything more, there was a great clattering of hooves from outside. They all three tensed; the hooves came to a halt, and the butler hurried to open the front doors. Before he could say anything, a tall figure swept past him and strode toward the stairs. It was Master Simon, his face grim and grey, his jaw very set.

"Papa." Quincy ran to him, arms outstretched.

Master Simon didn't even look at him. He simply reached out and shoved Quincy aside, so that the child crumpled gently to the floor, looking up at his father's retreating back with tears streaming down his cheeks. Master Simon strode up the stairs and disappeared.

"That's it. We've all had enough of your naughtiness," barked Miss Hardwick. She seized Quincy by the ear, making him shriek in pain. "Come with me at once."

Quincy was dragged away, and, hungry, tired, hardly knowing what else to do, Ada wandered down to the kitchens to help with the preparations for lunch.

Maybe she would be able to sneak out some scraps while she worked.

IT WAS to Ada's great relief that Cookie assigned her the task of slicing the stale bread to make bread pudding with supper. She took the opportunity immediately to cut off the heel and stuff it into her mouth, blowing on the fresh, hot bread as she did so. It was the first thing she'd eaten all day, and the simple act of filling her belly came as a great relief. Ada tried not to see how much her hands were shaking as she tore off small pieces of the bread and ate it.

She was licking the last crumbs from her fingers when the housekeeper strode over to the kitchen. Her eyes rested immediately on Ada, who froze to the spot. The housekeeper's eyes narrowed. "What are you doing with that bread, Miss Carter?"

"S-slicing it, ma'am," Ada stammered out. She had never lied before, but it came with surprising ease when she was hungry and trying her best to avoid punishment. It was so terrifying to feel alone. Her fingers closed around the handle of the breadknife, and she cut off a slice as though to demonstrate.

The housekeeper's eyes were still narrow. "Humph," she grunted, turning away to check on the stock in the pantry.

Ada slowly continued slicing the bread. The movement of the blade was strangely soothing, especially in a world where nothing made sense anymore. Mama had abandoned her to nurse Sophia, Quincy was torn away from everyone who gave him comfort, Master Simon had hurried back home but paid his son no mind. Things were cast into such turmoil, and –

The cry that came from upstairs was a sound that seemed almost inhuman. It was an eerie, echoing wail that made goosebumps rise all over Ada's body, a scream that was half animal and half phantasm, as though it was the dread offspring of the whine of a wounded dog and the screech of a restless ghost driven from the grave. Worst of all, Ada knew whose voice had uttered it, surely and instantly.

*Mama.*

Throwing down the breadknife, Ada bolted through the kitchen and up the stairs, taking two steps at a bound as she raced toward Sophia's room. The house was horribly silent. Her feet were slapping on the carpet, her breath was racing in her ears, and for a long few moments, it seemed as though the hallway was only getting longer and longer. Then she reached Sophia's room, and her heart fell to her feet like a stone. The doctors were all gathered around the doorway, their faces drawn and sombre. Master Simon was standing right in the doorway itself, his small, soft hands hanging down by his sides, useless and defeated. And from within the bedroom came the sound of Mama sobbing in a way that Ada had never heard her cry before. There was absolute hopelessness in it; a wrenching, wholehearted despair that horrified her.

"Mama?" Ada gasped, heedless of the important men around her. She shoved one of the doctors and Master Simon out of the way and crashed into the bedroom.

The sight of the room would be branded forever on her mind.

Cloths, basins, medicine bottles, medical equipment were scattered all over the room. Rumpled blankets lay on the floor; there was a layer of dust on every surface, the curtains drawn, the air musty with neglect. The bed was particularly chaotic, its covers drawn back and thrown down all over the place, rucked and crumpled on and around the bed.

And among it all, silent, unmoving, unbelievably pale, lay Sophia. She wore only a white linen slip, which was itself twisted and wrinkled, pulling up over one knee so that a shockingly white leg and foot lay naked on top of the covers. Ada stared at the leg. She had never seen Sophia's legs before, or anyone's, except for her own and Mama's.

"Oh, Sophie, Sophie, my one friend," Mama sobbed. "My one true friend."

Ada's eyes dragged upwards. The outline of Sophia's body seemed angular under her nightie, as though she had been reduced to nothing but bones. Her arms were two thin sticks on the covers, and her head was tipped back on the pillow, mouth open, eyes closed, motionless. Completely motionless.

Ada couldn't move.

Mama was lying half across the bed, her head on Sophia's chest, hugging and hugging her as though the sheer force of her love would restart the beating of Sophia's heart. Her words dissolved into wrenching sobs.

"I'm sorry, Mr. Morgan," said one of the doctors. "We did all we could."

Sophia Morgan was dead.

# CHAPTER 5

ADA COULDN'T UNDERSTAND why Mama hadn't been invited to the funeral. She was Sophia's best friend, after all. Ada had always known that Mama and Sophia were closer than most sisters, sharing some kind of deep bond that transcended class. If Sophia would have wanted anyone at her funeral, it would have been Mama.

Instead, they had to stand outside the cemetery, huddled under Mama's umbrella as a thin, misty rain drove against their faces, just enough so that Ada could hardly see the coffin being lowered into the great black hole in the earth. When the grave was filled in, there was a mound of naked earth over it. It seemed like a scar in the dirt somehow. Ada found herself wishing that green grass would grow fast over it. She thought that Sophia would like to lie under a blanket of green grass somehow, much better than just being buried, like something worthless, or perhaps like a seed. Ada couldn't quite decide which.

They waited until the crowd of people in black had dispersed before Mama led her around to the gate of the cemetery. Somehow, Ada thought, as she followed her mother toward the gate, it almost felt like Mama was lying in that grave as well. The woman walking beside her was less like her mother than like a reanimated corpse. Her face was very grey and tight, and she had hardly spoken since Sophia had died. She held Ada's hand, but the grip felt stiff and mechanical.

They walked over to the fresh grave. In the rain, the earth smelt strangely nice, considering that there were dead bodies in it. Mama let go of Ada's hand and crouched down to touch her palm to the elaborate marble headstone. *Sophia Louise Morgan, Beloved Wife and Mother, 1845-1874*. Ada wondered why the headstone didn't include *Beloved Friend* as well. She doubted Master Simon had ever loved Sophia the way Mama loved her.

Now, though, Mama didn't cry. She just closed her eyes and sat very still for a long moment, as though she herself had turned to marble. Then she got to her feet and took Ada's hand again, but there was no warmth in her grasp.

"Come, Ada," she said, her voice husky and dry, nothing like her usual voice at all.

They walked home, Ada and the ghost of her mother.

WHEN THEY WALKED into the kitchen at home, the butler was waiting there for him. He had a long, mournful face like a hound's, but his red eyes glittered now with something that might have been malice. Mama stopped dead the moment she looked into his face.

"What is it?" she asked.

Ada saw the butler smile for the first time. "Mr. Morgan wishes to speak with you," he said gravely. "I will conduct you to his study."

Mama swallowed hard. "Right after the funeral of his own wife?"

The butler's eyes turned steely. "Mr. Morgan wishes to see you *now*."

"Very well." Mama let out a shaky breath. "You stay here, Ada."

"Both of you," added the butler. "Your daughter is employed here as a housemaid, is she not?"

Mama stared at the butler, and Ada stared at Mama. This was all nonsense. She had never been a maid; she'd just been Quincy's friend, ever since she could remember. Sophia would never have considered her a maid. Would she?

Mama's shoulders slumped in defeat. "Yes," she said, in a small, broken voice. "She is. Come, Ada."

Ada's heart was suddenly pounding in her throat. She was shaking as she followed Mama and the butler out of the kitchen, up the stairs and into Master Simon's study. Just days ago, she'd peered through this keyhole, giggling as Quincy put glue into the ink of his father's pen. Now, there was no Quincy, and Master Simon wasn't writing. He was sitting behind his desk with his fingertips touching and his eyes dark as they rested on Mama and Ada.

"Miss Carter," he said, his tone icy. His eyes flitted to Ada. "*Both* Misses Carter."

"Yes, sir," said Mama, but her voice was tiny and tremulous.

The housekeeper was standing in the corner of the study, her chin up. Her eyes gleamed with something that frightened Ada. It was somewhere between smugness and delight, but there was nothing good or joyful about it. Instead, it sent an icy chill down Ada's spine.

Master Simon leaned forward. "Mrs. Hull here has informed me that you both are thieves," he said. "You are immediately dismissed. That will be all."

Ada felt a wave of relief. She wasn't sure why Mrs. Hull would say that they were thieves, since they clearly weren't, but Master Simon clearly wanted them to go out of his study. She turned, but Mama had frozen like a pillar of salt, and her face was very pale. The sight of it sent a jolt of pure fear through Ada's veins.

"Dismissed?" Mama breathed.

"Yes," said Master Simon. "I shall have no thieves in my house. Gather your things. You have one hour to leave this house, or I shall call the police."

"But sir," Mama cried. "We've never stolen anything – anything."

Master Simon leaned forward still more, his eyes growing intense.

"Mrs. Hull personally witnessed your daughter taking a heel of bread from the kitchen."

Mama blanched.

"I hadn't had breakfast yet," Ada protested. "I hadn't had anything to eat in days. Mrs. Hull feeds all the other servants, but not me."

"Did you have express permission to take that bread, Miss Carter?" demanded Mrs. Hull sharply.

Ada's heart sank. "N-no, ma'am."

"Then you stole it," said Master Simon. "Mrs. Hull has also witnessed you taking food from my late wife many times."

Mama was staring at him. "Sir, she always shared with me. It was her choice."

"Clothing, too," Mrs. Hull said quickly. "I've seen her take clothing."

"Sophia always gave me her old clothes." Mama's eyes were full of tears, her hands shaking.

"You're a thief and a liar, and you wormed your way into her life to the expense of the rest of us," Mrs. Hull snapped.

"Wormed. *Wormed?*" Mama burst out. Her voice rose to a pitch that Ada had never heard from her before. "I saved her life, and the life of your son besides. We became friends, true friends, in sweat and blood. Sophia was my rock, the only person who ever loved me, and we would have given everything for one another."

Tears were coursing down Mama's cheeks; Master Simon sat behind the desk, looking speechless.

"Sophia was a sister to me, the family I never had. She sought refuge in my arms when she knew that your love, such as it once was, had gone cold."

"ENOUGH!" Master Simon lunged to his feet. "Begone with you both, before I set the dogs on you."

He thundered the words with one arm upraised and pointing to the door. Mama stared at him for a few more moments, shaking visibly. Then she grabbed Ada's arm. "Come. We're going," she croaked.

"Going? Going where?" Ada asked, totally confused.

Mama half dragged her out of the study and down the hall.

"Away from here," she whispered. "Away from this house... and its ghosts."

"What ghosts, Mama?"

Mama was walking very quickly. Ada heard the slam of the study door; then they were hastening down the steps, toward the kitchen.

"Mama, you're frightening me," Ada cried. "Stop pulling. You're hurting me. I don't understand. Why are we going away? When will we come back?"

"We're never coming back, Ada," Mama snapped.

Ada stopped, wrenching her arm from Mama's grip. "But this is our home." she cried. "And Quincy is my friend. How will I ever see him again?"

Mama stared at her. There were still fresh tears on her cheeks, and her eyes were utterly despairing.

"This was never our home. Just a place we stayed." Her voice was brusque. "And sooner or later, Ada, Quincy would have realized that he can't be friends with you. He's rich, and you're not. That's just the way it is."

Mama's words sliced Ada's heart. She took a trembling step backwards. "No. No." she cried. "You always said that we're all people just the same. You always said not to think I was less important just because I was a maid's daughter. You always..."

"I was wrong." Mama barked. "We are less important, Ada, and that's just how it is." Her voice rose to a shriek.

Ada stumbled back. She couldn't face this. She wanted Quincy, she *needed* Quincy. He was the only one who would understand now.

She wheeled around and bolted up the steps, heading for the nursery.

"Ada, get back here," Mama shouted.

Ada had no intention of going back to her mother. She kept running, bounding up the stairs, onto the landing, down the hall – and straight into Quincy. They grabbed one another's arms to keep from falling over and spun around, almost tripping over one another.

"Ada," Quincy cried.

"Quin." Ada clung to him, looking desperately into his soft eyes. They were red with tears. "You have to help me. Help me."

"Ada!" Mama thundered.

"Your father dismissed us," Ada panted. "He wants to chase us out of the house."

"*No.*" Quincy's hands tightened on her arms. "You're my only friend, Ada."

"Master Quincy, come here at once," roared his governess.

Mama had reached the top of the stairs. She was storming toward Ada, her eyes strangely blank and hollow and devoid of emotion. "Ada, come. We're leaving," she said coldly.

"No, Elsie, no," Quincy cried out. Fresh tears washed down his cheeks. "Don't go."

"Ada, come!" Mama barked, grabbing Ada's arm.

"Don't. No. No," Ada shrieked.

The governess had appeared, and she seized Quincy's hair. He let out a scream but didn't let go of Ada.

"Please don't go," he sobbed. "Don't go."

"Quincy," Ada howled, but Mama was pulling too hard. She couldn't hold onto Quincy's arm. It slipped through her fingers, and she was being dragged away, and Quincy was screaming and screaming.

But there was nothing she could do.

# PART II

# CHAPTER 6

*Two Years Later*

It was March already, but London still seemed stuck in the throes of January. Ada placed her feet carefully as she walked, avoiding the black ice that coated many of the stones on the pavement in this part of the city. It was hard enough to walk here at the best of times, what with all the missing paving-stones and the miscellaneous rubbish that littered the streets. This early in the morning, with so much of the ground still frozen, it was almost impossible to walk without slipping.

At least there was no wind today. Just a bone-deep chill, a creeping and insidious thing, oozing out of the air, through the threadbare surface of Ada's inadequate coat, and down into her flesh. It seemed to be sucking the very life out of her bones. Not that there had been much life to begin with when she'd risen this morning, her belly aching with hunger, her feet with cold.

Around her, the streets began to change for the better. She walked quickly, knowing that it wouldn't be long before the morning crowds began to move through the streets on whatever errands they pleased. Even though Ada slipped out of the tenement just after six o' clock – the time at which Mama left for work – she was still only just going to make it to the square by half past seven. It was a long and treacherous walk through the city, which was another reason why Mama would have a fit if she knew where Ada was really going every day.

The weight of that deception weighed on Ada's shoulders. But she reassured herself with the thought that at least people were slightly more generous here. It was better for Mama, too, that she came to beg here. Perhaps that made the lying all right.

She pulled her coat a little more tightly around her shoulders as she walked up to the familiar marketplace. There was something deeply soothing about the square, and it wasn't just because of its beauty, although it certainly was one of the loveliest places in all of London. The cobblestones had been there for generations; there were gentle archways everywhere, ornate wrought-iron lampposts gleaming in the dark morning, the shops all just beginning to wake, with happy shopkeepers calling out cheerful greetings despite the cold that sucked at

Ada's spirit. Yet it was not just the beauty of it that soothed her. It was the familiarity. This was the marketplace where, as little as two years ago, Mama and Sophia and Ada had often gone shopping together. Sophia would never go to the millinery without her lady's maid, and Ada often got to tag along. She'd have to sit very quietly and obediently in a corner, and the milliner and seamstresses were often snide with her. But she always enjoyed it anyway.

Now, she gazed with longing at the millinery. Those memories felt a lifetime ago, almost as if they'd happened to someone else, someone who hadn't known what it was to be hungry or cold. Not the way she was hungry and cold right now as she cupped her hands together and dragged her eyes away from the millinery, focusing instead on the crowds hurrying past.

As always, the crowds here were mostly wealthy. The poorest of them passed by her now on their way to work, but even they wore warm clothing and had rosy cheeks: housekeepers and stablemasters, clerks and artisans, plumbers and carpenters. People who had a few pennies to spare.

A few pennies were all that Ada wanted.

She held out her hands, pitching her voice higher, bending a little at the knees to seem smaller. This had been much easier when she was eleven rather than thirteen.

"Alms?" she cried out softly, her voice pathetic against the bitter cold and darkness. "Please, sir, spare a penny for the poor?"

The portly gentleman brushing past her had his eyes trained on a brightly polished pocket-watch, and hardly looked up as he passed. Ada might as well not have existed.

"It's cold, and I haven't a penny to my name," she said, her voice plaintive without any added effort. "I just need a bit of coal. Please, a few pennies for a little coal?"

A young lady paused, digging in her pocket. She produced a farthing and dropped it into Ada's hands without looking at her.

"Oh, thank you, miss, thank you kindly," said Ada.

The young woman didn't look around. Ada tucked away the penny, trying not to feel ungrateful for it, but almost willing to trade it just for a moment's eye contact or a smile. She cupped her hands again, pushing away the thought.

"Alms for the poor? Any alms?" she called out.

Her voice was thin and reedy against the rising hustle of the waking city. The shop doors were opening now, people coming inside, the chime of doorbells ringing down the street. A gaggle of schoolchildren scampered past in their long socks, giggling, and clutching their books close. Ada wished for a real book in her hands again. She didn't think she'd even touched a book since she'd been torn away from the Morgan house, and from Quincy.

"Spare a penny for a hungry child, sir?" she pleaded, holding out her hand to a gentleman with bushy gray whiskers.

He stopped, his eyes raking her. There was something horrible about the way they dwelled on the new curves of her body, curves that she herself was not yet comfortable with. He seemed to take pleasure in them in a way that made her skin crawl.

"Why, you're hardly a child, are you?" he said, his voice growing husky as he leaned a little closer.

Ada recoiled. This was not the first man who had said something to this effect in the past few weeks. "I'm thirteen," she protested.

He shrugged, turned away. "Almost old enough," he murmured.

*Old enough for what?* Ada wasn't sure she wanted to know the answer to that question. She turned away again, distracting herself by scanning through the crowd, although she was doing so with far less enthusiasm than when she'd first plucked up the courage to return to the marketplace where she'd been so happy. Her eyes caught every youthful, boyish face, but of course, none of them were Quincy's. Why would they be? He was the young master of the house; shopping was no business of his. Ada didn't think he'd been down to this particular marketplace more than five or six times in the years she could remember.

She tried to keep hoping. But with the farthing in her pocket, the hunger in her belly, and the cold in her bones, hope was almost as difficult to afford as courage.

THE BAG of coal bounced on Ada's back, a tiny triumph, especially in combination with the few potatoes she'd thrust into her pocket. There were three of them, one and a half each for her and for Mama, and they weren't even green or wrinkled or mouldy. The vegetable seller had been in a hurry to get home and had given them to Ada for a good price. Perhaps she and Mama would even be able to sleep tonight without hunger pangs assailing their stomachs.

It all depended on whether Mama's boss had been happy with her at work. When he was, he'd give her the leftover bits of fish, and she could boil them down into a kind of watery soup. But if he wasn't satisfied, he would give her nothing. Maybe not even wages. And if he hadn't paid her...

Ada tried not to think about the consequences. She was almost too tired to think at all, only to plod forward, one foot after the other. The cobblestones and new-fangled tar had given way to mud, and there was a slow drizzle falling, an embarrassed and ineffectual thing that made Ada's clothes cling to her body. Around her, the stench of poverty rose thickly from the gaping windows of rundown houses, slapped together on the cheap and then left to rot. Noisome alleyways were populated with piles of silent, bony people, their eyes hollow and distant in a world filled with the mad visions of opium.

Ada was fairly sure that most of the people in the tenement used opium, too, judging by the wails and strange mutterings that she and Mama heard at night sometimes. But it was a roof over their heads, at least, even if they lived on the ground floor, and in the back room where rain tended to leak in through the gaps of the thin brick walls and made black mould bloom morbidly in one corner. The latrine door was right opposite theirs. Ada held her breath against the unspeakable stench as she approached the flaking front door.

"It's me, Mama," she called out.

There was a deep sigh from within by way of reply. Ada pushed the door open and stepped inside, then shut the door to seal out at least some of the appalling reek from the latrine. Truth be told, the tenement itself didn't smell much better. The black mould in the corner contributed a quiet, underlying, fungal smell to everything, as musty and horrible as the glistening surface of the mould itself. There was a pallet in the opposite corner, covered by a few blankets, both moth-eaten and threadbare. Mama sat in the final corner, huddled around the tiny excuse for a fireplace even though no fire burned there. Ada's eyes flashed over her mother, but she instantly noticed that there was no newspaper-wrapped parcel with her, and her heart sank even before she could take in the usual details telling the story of a long and painful day at the docks. Mama's hands were withered and bent in her lap, sore and reddened from hours of cleaning fish. Her eyes were reddened, distant; she seemed to look through Ada instead of at her. Ada wondered if Sophia would even be able to recognize Mama now. But the thought of Sophia was far too sad. She would have been heartbroken to see Mama in this state.

"He didn't let me have the fish," said Mama in a small voice. She lowered her eyes to the floor. "I'm sorry, Ada. It wasn't even my fault. One of the sailors came past, got handsy with me..." She looked away.

Ada sometimes longed for the days when Mama would protect her from dreadful truths. "It's all right," she said. "I brought potatoes, and two apples. They're only the least bit wrinkled."

Mama managed a smile. "Thank you, dear."

"And I have a few sticks of firewood, too."

Mama brightened still more. "There we are, then. We'll eat the apples while you boil the potatoes."

"Did..." Ada paused. "Did he give you your wages today, Mama?"

"Yes, darling. We'll be all right for rent on Monday."

Ada let out a breath. At first, she had been appalled that any landowner could dream of charging rent for the dubious privilege in living in this cold, unhealthy space, but after one awful week before Mama had found the job, she had learned that there was nothing worse than being on the streets. Even this tenement was the lap of luxury by comparison.

"How did you go?" asked Mama. "It must have been good, if you could bring both wood and potatoes."

"It was fine, Mama."

Mama gave her a shrewd, worrying look. "Where did you say you'd gone begging today?"

"On the edge of Whitechapel, Mama," lied Ada, her heart thudding painfully in her chest. "Near the churches there."

"I see," said Mama quietly. "Strange those people were so generous today."

Ada couldn't think of anything to say, so she said nothing. She tipped the potatoes into the pot of cold water and set it over the fire, then she started packing out the firewood. Small movements. Small tasks. She could survive all this, if she broke it down into small things, and tried to forget that she had spent yet another day staring through the crowds for Quincy and had gone yet another day without finding him.

And if she prayed, constantly, incessantly, for a strength she thought she might never have.

# CHAPTER 7

D<small>AYS</small> like these were the worst when it came to begging.

Ada huddled in the locked doorway of an empty house, trying to draw as much as possible of herself into the tiny lee to avoid the driving rain that was coming down in sheets. It was so cold, and so whipped by the wind, that each droplet felt like a shard of glass being thrust into her skin.

The few people on the roads today were all hurrying home with their hoods pulled up over their heads, muffled and focused only on their own feet, their own rush, their own mad dash toward home. Ada wondered what lovely things awaited most of the people hurrying by on this square. Food and fireplaces, dry clothes, perhaps even a hot bath. She remembered a time when she and Quincy had been soaked by rain while playing in the park one afternoon. His governess had hurried them home, to Mama's and Sophia's arms, and they'd both been towelled vigorously and put down in front of the fire with warm, dry clothes, blankets around them, and cups of chocolate.

Ada leaned her head back against the door, smiling at the memory even as a knot of tears clogged her throat. There would be no chocolate or fireplaces or towels for her today. It was noon, and she hadn't made a single penny, nor did she expect to make any today. Everyone was far too busy thinking about their own inconveniences to be worried about some little beggar girl crumpled up in a doorway.

She gazed idly at the people, holding out her hands from time to time with a quiet plea, even though she hated the sudden gust of cold and rain on her outstretched hands. Most of them seemed so annoyed with one another; governesses tugging children along in their raincoats and wellies, husbands and wives hurrying side-by-side as they argued, silent groups of workers plodding past without a word. Among them all, an old woman was lost in the rain and chaos. She was clearly well-off; a sturdy umbrella over her head, a leather purse under her arm, her clothes warm, but nonetheless she moved in small, painful, shuffling steps toward the cab that had stopped on the corner, presumably for her.

She looked as though she might pass right by Ada, and Ada sat up, not sure if she wanted to offer her an arm or just beg for some money. Maybe the old woman would give her money out of gratitude if she helped her. Feeling guilty for the thought, Ada started forward, but at that moment a stray cat came darting across the pavement. Ears flat, rain flying from its coat, it rushed right in front of her, and the old woman tripped. With a cry of alarm, she fell, purse and umbrella flying, hands and knees into the gutter.

Before Ada could get to her feet, there was the sound of running footsteps splashing in the rain. A boy about her own age crouched down beside the old woman, grasping her arm. "Let's get you up, ma'am," he said cheerfully.

Something about that voice... It was familiar, but wrong somehow, like hearing Mama's voice distorted through the echoes of an old, empty building, like the abandoned warehouse where they'd spent a few nights right after being dismissed from the Morgan house.

The old woman clutched at him. "Oh, dear boy, dear boy," she wheezed ineffectually.

The boy tugged her to her feet, brushing the mud from her skirt, and gathered up her purse and umbrella in one movement. "Here you are," he said. "Can I hail you a cab, ma'am?"

"No – no, there's one right over there, waiting for me," said the old woman. She grabbed his arm. "Oh – this rain is frightening."

"Don't worry," said the boy. "Let me walk you there."

They headed off, an odd couple, the bent little old woman, the tall figure of the boy. Ada squinted at him, a strange suspicion rising in her chest. But it couldn't be... surely not. It was just her hunger and cold that was making her imagine what she really wanted, more than anything, more than anything else in the entire world.

The boy had escorted the old woman to the cab now, and with a lot of twittering and patting his head, she was scrambling inside. He held the door for her politely, then closed it and turned around, and for the first time Ada saw his face.

A dear, dear face, so precious, so kind, the eyes so warm, the smile so easy, a face she'd looked into so many times over the years, the face of someone who had become the only friend she had, the only friend she needed –

She wanted to call out Quincy's name. She wanted to run to him and grab his hands the way she'd always done when they were small children. She found her feet, and his eyes darted toward her as though noticing her for the first time. He'd see her. They were going to be reunited at last. It was finally happening.

"QUINCY!" thundered a voice.

Ada's blood turned to ice. *Master Simon.*

She cringed back into the doorway, cowering in the shadows as the tall figure of her erstwhile master came striding down the street. Quincy whipped around, cowering where he stood, his fear more familiar than his now-deep voice.

"What are you doing?" Master Simon thundered, grabbing Quincy's arm roughly.

"I – I was just helping this lady – " Quincy began.

"I ordered you to stay by my side," Master Simon snapped. "Now stay by my side, or so help me, child, I'll take my belt to you right here on this street."

Quincy's voice sounded thick with tears. "Yes, Papa. I'm sorry, Papa."

Master Simon gave him a nasty shake that made Ada stumble forward out of her doorway, hand outstretched as though to grab Quincy and pull him away from his father's cruelty. That was when he saw her. His eyes widened when they rested on her, and for a moment, an expression of utter joy transfixed his terrified face. He looked like the little boy who had been her best friend again, and Ada would have cried out to him if she had not been absolutely breathless with joy.

"Come, boy." Master Simon barked. "Our carriage just around the corner."

He pulled Quincy around and stormed away, dragging his son after him. Quincy looked back twice. The first time, Ada started forward again, but he gave a tiny shake of his head – *No.* Before she could puzzle out what it meant, he disappeared around the corner with his father, looking back one last time. There were tears running down his cheeks.

ADA WAS SO busy staring into the crowd that she nearly forgot to beg at all.

It was silly, she supposed, considering that she had been coming here for a long time and seen Quincy just once. The chances of seeing him again must be vanishingly small. Besides, it had been a week since she'd seen him, and there had been no sign of him or Master Simon.

Yet still, hope bubbled in her heart, especially on a day as lovely as this one. It seemed as though the city had finally realized it was spring, and the sun was pouring richly down onto the square, holding some of the golden warmth of the approaching summer. Ada's coat was finally drying out for the first time in days. She relished the feeling of not being cold, and all the time her eyes probed the crowd, searching and searching for a familiar face, a smile that made everything seem better.

Her vantage point, at least, was perfect for searching the crowd – if not for begging. The little alley was hidden right in the corner of the market square, serving as a place for the bakery on one side and the tailor on the other to put their bins. Few people actually passed by here, but Ada could see everyone walking through the square clearly. If Quincy came here today – and she knew that her *if* held an astounding amount of unlikelihood – she'd see him.

She was almost startled when there was the quiet chink of two coins in her palm. Looking down at them for a moment, she felt her heart leap. Half-a-crown. It was more money than she made in a week sometimes. She started down at the coins for a few moments, then slowly raised her face to look at her benefactor.

He was young, and for a wild instant, Ada thought that it might be Quincy. But there was nothing of Quincy in this young man's eyes. They were like two cold black pebbles at the bottom of a lake, hard and mysterious, and there was an ugly scar that split the corner of his bottom lip in a sharp white line. Ada recoiled almost without meaning to.

"Th-thank you, s-sir," she stammered out.

He leered at her in a way that curdled her insides. "There, you've had your payment," he said, taking a step closer. There was an appalling, sour reek to his breath that made nausea rise in her chest. She recognized within it the potential to keep her alive, the thing that had kept her alive through many encounters just like this one in the past few weeks and reacted on instinct. Her right knee lurched up, meeting its mark with a sharpness that made the man stumbled back with a howl of pain.

Ada didn't wait to see if anyone came to her aid. No one would; that much the past two years had taught her. Whirling around, she shoved past him and into the street, bolting.

"Get back here!" he howled. "You cheap hussy."

Ada remembered the smell on his breath and knew she could outrun him. Ducking under a stationary grocer's cart, she bolted down one street, then up the next, then doubled back into the other side of the square and hid behind a flower-seller's cart. It wasn't long before she saw the man blundering past, still bow-legged and bent over, cursing furiously.

Ada let out a slow, aching sigh. One thing was clear: begging was no longer as comparatively safe as it once had been.

She would need to think of another way.

THE SIGN in the apothecary's window was small and handwritten, but the words on it leaped out to grab Ada's eye, confirming what she'd read in the advertisement in the papers. *Clerk position at busy apothecary. Only intelligent, well-educated, pretty and presentable young ladies need apply.* The sign in the window was far less eloquent: CLERK WANTED. Both of them seemed, to Ada, to be bursting with promise.

She took a deep breath, smoothed down her dress, and pushed open the door. She'd specifically chosen ten o' clock on a Tuesday to come to the apothecary; it would be quiet then, and she'd have better luck talking to the owner. A balding man with little round glasses stood behind the counter. Dipping his chin, he glared at her over his glasses when she came in.

"I don't have any opium for the likes of you," he snapped.

"I beg your pardon, sir, but I do not require any opium," said Ada smoothly. She'd been practicing her enunciation quietly on street corners when she tried begging in between looking for work; it was the only way for her and Mama to have enough money for both food and rent. Still, the syllables felt sloppy compared to the way that they used to back when she was sitting in on Quincy's daily lessons. "I have come here to enquire about the clerk position that you advertised in Sunday morning's paper."

The man narrowed his eyes. Ada imagined that he was Mr. Reading, the man whose name was over the shop door.

"I don't like your tone, girl," he snapped, his eyes traveling briskly up and down her raggedy dress. "In fact, I don't like anything about you. Get out of my shop."

"Sir, please," Ada protested. "I can read, write, and cipher, and I can add and multiply, and do all the things necessary for this position. I would – "

"I told you to get out, street urchin," shouted the apothecary, reaching under the counter and extricating a small, deadly-looking club. "Get out."

Ada backed away, despair rising in her heart as she hurriedly exited the shop and darted into the alley across the street. This was the fourth time she'd tried to find work, and she'd learned to plan her escape routes, no matter how well-spoken she thought she sounded. It was as if the sight of her rags rendered people immediately both blind and deaf to everything else about her.

She sank down onto an old wooden box in the alley, letting out a deep sigh of despair. Mama had always told her to keep reading the bits of newspapers she brought home wrapped around the fish, that her education would do her good someday. It seemed, though, that her education didn't count one bit to prospective employers.

Ada glanced up and down the street, looking for a good nearby corner where she could beg and at least make up enough money to buy a bit of stale bread so that they wouldn't go hungry tonight. She knew Mama wouldn't be angry even if she didn't succeed. That was the frightening part. Mama wouldn't be pleased, or angry, or sad, or anything. It seemed as though Mama was floating through the world without actually touching it, a ghost impenetrable to any emotion except her own inner turmoil.

These dark thoughts so filled Ada's mind that she almost didn't see the girl in blue until she'd reached the door of the apothecary. The girl was slim and lovely; her dress was nowhere near the rich beauty that Sophia's had always been, but was obviously new, hanging neatly around her figure. Her hair was piled up on top of her head and secured there with a large bone clip.

Ada crept a little nearer. This girl must be applying to the job, too, and if she succeeded, maybe Ada would learn something – and have better luck next time.

As soon as the door closed behind the girl, Ada hurried to the open window to listen, keeping her head down in the hopes that the apothecary wouldn't see her.

"Good morning," said the girl cheerfully. "I'm here about the job."

Ada snorted to herself. Surely this poor girl had to know that she didn't stand a chance of getting the job if her speech was going to be so uncouth.

"Why, good morning, young lady," said the apothecary, his voice completely different – sweet as pie. "What's your name?"

Ada's jaw dropped. She stared through the window openly, shocked to see that the young lady was slouching on the counter, her shoulders slumped, yet the apothecary was regarding her with a warm, approving smile.

"Rae Higgs, sir, and it's a pleasure to meet you," said the girl. "I can read, write and do a bit of arithmetic; nothing too diffi-cult, but a bit of adding and such, like."

"Well, you are a very presentable young lady," said the apothe-cary approvingly.

Fifteen minutes later, Rae Higgs was hired. And Ada was watching her walk away with a spring in her step. Ada's heart burned with anger and perceived injustice. How could Rae have gotten that job, despite being clearly so much less educated than Ada was?

The clouds parted slightly, and a flash of sunshine sparkled on Rae's dress. There was nothing fancy about it, but its nicely cut material was evident.

Ada narrowed her eyes. *Presentable*. The apothecary wasn't concerned over finding an educated girl; he wanted a neat, tidy, and well-dressed one.

Her heart ached within her. Intelligence was cheaper.

# CHAPTER 8

MAMA ATE IN SILENCE. They usually did; it was such a battle of will to eat slowly. Ada always wanted to wolf down every morsel, but on a night like tonight, it was especially important for her to relish every bite. There weren't many.

She carefully scraped out the last dregs of gruel from her tin bowl, sucking hungrily at the spoon when it was all gone. Tonight's portion had been even smaller than usual. She was painfully aware that begging was growing less and less profitable for her.

Looking up at Mama over the rim of her bowl, she saw that her mother was staring down into her own empty bowl as if she had no idea where the food could possibly have gone. Mama's eyes were glassy with exhaustion, her face slack and blank, as if she couldn't muster the muscular effort to either smile or frown. Ada knew what she was worrying about, too. They were getting to a point where they had to choose between food and rent.

"It's going to be all right, Mama," said Ada.

Mama let out a long, slow sigh. "Yes, darling," she said, barely listening. Slowly, stiffly, she got to her feet. Ada noticed how chapped and bruised her hands were tonight, and her heart stung with empathy. She rose, taking the bowl from her mother, and took them both over to the enamel basin in the corner that they used for the washing-up.

"No, really, Mama," she said, plunging the two bowls into the basin. "I think I've come up with a way to make things better."

Mama was sitting on the pallet, slowly and painfully taking her shoes off. Ada knew that underneath, her toes were reddened and misshapen, all calluses and squashed toenails. They must hurt so much. Ada's heart stung for her.

"That would be nice," said Mama quietly, stripping off her damp socks and putting them to one side.

"I stopped by the apothecary's for that job I told you about, remember?" said Ada. She paused. "I'm afraid I didn't get it."

Part of her still expected – perhaps even hoped – that Mama would be disappointed by that news. Or sad, or angry – or just react to it in any way at all. Instead, Mama simply nodded vaguely. "That's all right," she mumbled.

"Then another girl came in and got the job," said Ada. "And she wasn't half as educated as I am, Mama. But she was much better *dressed*. So I think I can still get a job – a good one, too, one where I can get us out of this dreadful old tenement."

Mama was stifling a yawn as she stretched herself out on the pallet, eyes already beginning to close.

"That would be nice, dear," she whispered.

"I just need to dress better," said Ada. "I need to wash my hair and do something with it, and smell a little better, and most of all, I need a better dress."

She turned, the dishes done, to gauge Mama's reaction. But it was already too late for that. Mama lay with her head tipped back, eyes blissfully closed, sleeping. She had been awake for about thirty minutes since coming home, and that was that. Ada knew she would wake just before work and leave again without saying more than a few words to Ada.

Loneliness ran through her like a knife. She felt as though Mama, the vibrantly happy Mama she had grown up with, lay in the same grave as Sophia Morgan.

Letting out a soft sigh, she sat down on the pallet beside her mother, laying a hand on her shoulder.

"I'm going to make it better, Mama," she whispered. "Don't you worry. One way or the other... I'll make it all better. We'll have a better house, and I'll get to see Quincy. Maybe I'll even rescue him from his awful father. Won't that be nice?"

In response, Mama let out a long, deep sigh and tugged the blanket a little higher up on her shoulder. Ada squeezed her shoulder gently, then tucked the blanket around her mother.

She meant every word she'd said.

ADA COULDN'T BELIEVE her luck.

She had been standing in exactly the right place that morning when the baker was throwing away the morning's stale bread. It was just after another failed attempt at finding work, when she'd come to a nearby grocery in response to an advertisement looking for help. Of course, the grocer had taken one look at her rags and shouted at her that she was nothing more than a common thief.

She wasn't a thief, but she was certainly hungry as she stood in the street in front of the grocery, feeling utterly lost. Her legs ached; she'd started to go further and further afield in search of work, and food was growing more and more scarce as she focused on finding work rather than begging. Not that begging was much good anymore. It was summer now, and people had forgotten how cold and awful it was to be on the streets.

The baker had come out of his shop right about then with an armful of loaves: all white and lovely and clean, with not a speck of mould on them, but Ada guessed that they were stale. Unlike the baker back in the old marketplace where she'd seen Quincy, this one clearly didn't have any pigs. He carried the loaves out to a nearby rubbish bin and dumped then inside, then walked away, slapping his hands clean of crumbs.

Ada had had the lid off that bin before the door had closed behind the baker. One of the loaves was irreparably squashed and impossible to carry home, but there were two that were untouched, once she'd flicked some tomato peels and name-less dirt away from them. Tucking them both under her arm, she'd thought of the little park two blocks away that she'd passed on her way here. If she was going to have a glorious feast, she might as well enjoy it somewhere nice.

That was how she came to be sitting on a bench in a small, neat park, slowly eating an entire loaf of bread on her own. She would keep the other loaf for Mama in its entirety, of course, but for now it felt very good to sit in the sunshine and gulp down handful after handful of real, solid food.

The bench she'd chosen was off in one corner of the park, away from the rest, and for good reason. The other two benches – just on the other side of the small duck pond –

were occupied by young ladies. Governesses, Ada supposed, judging by the number of well-dressed children playing around at their feet.

Leaning back in her bench and relaxing a little, Ada found that the wind was gently blowing the governesses' quiet chatter across the pond toward her. The nearest was a dark-haired girl, indulgently watching three little girls playing with wildflowers in the soft grass. She was chatting with a scattered-looking redhead.

"I'm telling you, Lizzy, it's far nicer than that old job back down by the factory," the dark-haired girl was saying.

"Aren't the hours far longer, though?" asked the redhead, looking dubious. "At least the factories are down to twelve hours a day, and one gets Sundays off besides."

"Yes but think of how dreadful that air is for you," said Lizzy. "As for the pay – well. There's no comparison."

Ada sat up. *Pay?* The money wasn't terrible if one worked in a factory, but it sounded like being a governess was even better.

The redhead folded her arms. "Aren't the children awfully spoiled?"

"Well, yes, but that's the good thing – one can teach them to be more respectful. You don't have to put up with it," said Lizzy. "And I can use my education, which I couldn't do in a factory."

The redhead sighed. "If one is lucky enough to have an education."

Ada leaned forward. She did, and she was certain it was enough of an education to teach small children to read, write, and do a few sums. After all, she'd received the same tutoring as Quincy, which was far more than any woman really ought to know – at least, it was according to Quincy's tutor.

At that moment, one of the small children tripped and fell on his hands and knees. Letting out a dreadful squall, the child sat back and began to cry.

"Oh, Norman," cried Lizzy, jumping to her feet and hurrying toward him, effectively ending her conversation with the redhead. But Ada stayed where she was, slowly chewing her bread and staring at the girl. As the awful men on the street kept reminding her, Ada looked older than her thirteen years, even in rags. She knew she could pass as sixteen or so, which was old enough to be a governess.

*As for the pay, there's no comparison.*

Even a factory job would give Ada enough money to at least buy her mother food and maybe even help with the rent. Being a governess sounded even better, perhaps good enough to get Mama out of that dreadful tenement, even to allow her to stop working for that beastly man at the docks.

There was one great obstacle, however. Ada stared down at her ragged dress. She'd been so dismayed when she'd outgrown the sturdy dress she'd been wearing when Master Simon dismissed them. Mama had replaced it with a sad, cheap garment she'd bought from a shady-looking street-seller who had probably stolen it. It had worn so thin over her knees that she could see the fine mesh of her petticoat through the cloth, which had once been blue, but now faded to a pathetic ash grey. She reached up and fingered her dirty, matted locks, then looked up at Lizzy again. The girl's face was tastefully painted – just a touch of rouge and a little powder, nothing excessive. Her hair was shining with cleanliness and neatly braided down her back, and she wore a dress that was both practical and elegant, flowing easily over her slim body.

Ada thought of Rae Higgs and her nice dress and her uneducated speech. If she couldn't get a job at the apothecary dressed like this, she stood no chance as a governess. There were no two ways about it: Ada needed a better dress.

She could think of only one place where she might get one.

Ada had been very small the day that Sophia had offered Mama some of her old ball gowns, but she still remembered her awe when she watched Sophia taking the red one out of her wardrobe and lifting one edge of the skirt so that it fell open over her body, shimmering lace, gleaming silk, intricate embroidery. Everything about the dress had been beautiful, but Ada particularly remembered the way it had sounded. Its rustle was thick and musical, speaking of incredible softness and weight, of dancing.

Awestruck, young Ada had sat on a cushion in Sophia's dressing room while Mama reached out to finger the dress's swooping neckline. "Oh, Sophia, it's beautiful," she said softly.

"It's a little old-fashioned, isn't it?" said Sophia. "It's from my courting days." She laughed, giving a nostalgic little sigh, and turned to look at herself in the mirror. Her eyes grew misty, as though imagining better days. "Simon seemed so wonderful back then."

Mama made a disapproving sound in the back of her throat. She'd never liked Simon.

Sophia turned to Mama, her smile reappearing. "Well, it's certainly not going to fit me now – not after having Quincy. But look at you, Elsie. You're just a little slip of a thing. Why, it'll fit you perfectly."

She held it up against Mama, and Ada gasped in joy. With the red dress tumbling to the ground around her feet, and the long, draping sleeves hanging down by her sides, and her thick curls hanging in shining loops on her shoulders, Mama looked like a princess. No, more than a princess: a magnificent empress of some distant and exotic land.

"Oh, Mama, you're so beautiful," Ada had burst out.

Sophia laughed. "See? Ada approves."

"I couldn't, Sophie." Mama smiled, pushing the dress gently away. "Thank you, but it's just too beautiful. I don't have balls to go to. I'd have no use for it."

Sophia's face faltered, and she looked down at the dress. "I suppose you're right," she sighed. "I just wanted to give you something lovely."

"Your friendship is the loveliest thing I have," Mama had said.

So Sophia had called in an errand-boy, and told him to take the dress to "the mission house on Walden Street."

Ada's arms were wrapped around her body as she walked briskly through the unseasonably cold morning. It was heavily overcast, grey clouds lowering over the rooftops, and she thought it would soon be raining. Perhaps there would be more at the mission house than just gowns. Ada could only imagine that this mysterious mission house was some kind of place where rich people sent their old clothes for the poor, and if she didn't find an old ball gown there, maybe she'd at least find a decent-looking dress. And a coat. And a scarf for Mama. She had no idea if they'd sell these items or give them away or how it would work, but it was the only idea she had.

If only finding Walden Street was as easy as remembering its name. Ada had been searching for it for three long days, begging as she went, sometimes fearing she might have gotten lost, once only finding her way home long after dark. Mama had been furious then. Ada hadn't told her where she'd been all day, and that had only made her angrier, even though Ada had brought home some food. She knew that if she told Mama what risks she was taking in the faint hope of finding a better job... well, Mama might not even hear her. Mama hardly heard anything she said, these days. Sometimes Ada wished she would be a little angry again, or at least notice her.

She pushed that thought aside, pausing on a street corner, and looking left and right. So far, she'd searched about five blocks north, east, and south of the Morgan house. She couldn't think that Sophia would have sent an errand-boy much further than that. Now, she was heading west, but the streets here were a mad and senseless jumble. Some of them doubled back on one another; others curved so gently that she hardly noticed until she ended up right back where she started. Others were so crazed and crooked that they felt more like the tunnels of a rabbit warren than city streets.

Everywhere she went, though, she could smell the rotten air of neglect. The buildings were silent and bare, with boarded-up windows and fragments of tattered curtains that stirred quietly in the breeze. Dead-eyed drunks sat in the corners, gaping at her with slack mouths, their faces motionless. She saw a few children, but none of them were playing. They just sat around, staring at her with hollow eyes. One of them – not much more than a baby – was chewing hopelessly on a chicken bone that seemed to already be bleached white with the sun or with boiling.

She dared not speak to the drunks, and she figured the children wouldn't know, so she approached the only other person she could see: a listless woman who was leaning against the wall, smoking the butt of a cigarette with hungry, sucking breaths.

"Excuse me, ma'am?" she said.

The woman studied her. "Ma'am?" she sneered on a cloud of smoke. "Been a long time since anyone called me that." She blew out the rest of the smoke very slowly, almost regretfully, as though relishing its thick presence in her lungs.

"I'm sorry to trouble you," said Ada, "but..."

"Then why trouble me at all, you little toff?" snorted the woman. "Toff in rags, rather." She took a long drag at the cigarette, sucking so hard that her cheeks hollowed inward.

Ada took the opportunity to speak. "I was hoping to ask you for directions. I'm looking for the mission house on Walden Street."

The woman hissed out some smoke. "Hark at you," she chuckled. "What happened to you, with your fancy speech?" She gave a mock bow with a little flourish of her hand. "Fall on hard times, m'lady?"

Ada's eyes stung at the mockery. Would this woman treat her this way if she knew the truth? "Harder than you know." she cried. "Why, once I had everything, and now – "

"At least you had everything once." The woman straightened, her eyes suddenly very hard, her voice very flat. "Unlike those of us who will only always have nothing."

Ada didn't know what to say. "M-ma'am?"

The woman leaned forward, spitting the words on a cloud of smoke that went straight into Ada's eyes and lungs. "Get out of my sight."

Coughing, Ada stumbled back, more hurt by the words than the smoke. She turned around and hurried away, wiping at the tears in her eyes. She couldn't understand why no one would help her. It was still hard for her to grasp. All her life, Sophia and Quincy and Mama had been so ready to help her. Now, she felt she was completely on her own...

"Miss?"

Ada stopped. It was a little boy who had spoken; no older than ten or so, huddled among his siblings in the doorway of a tumbledown house.

"Yes?" she said, with all the grace she could manage; which, at that moment, wasn't much.

"You're looking for the mission house, are you?" the boy asked.

"Yes, I am," said Ada.

"Well, you're not far away. Just go down that street o'er there, and then take the second left and the first right, and it'll be on the corner. It's a big square building – you won't miss it." He paused, his eyes saddening. "My mama's in there. I won't ask why you have to go there, but I'm sorry."

Something about the way he said it made Ada's skin crawl. She wanted to ask him what the mission house really was, and why his mother was in there, but the look in his eyes warned her not to.

"Thank you," she said. "I wish I had something to give you."

The boy shrugged and turned away, clearly dismissing her. With trepidation rising in her heart, Ada headed in the direction he'd indicated.

# CHAPTER 9

THE SIGHT of the mission house sent a dreadful chill down Ada's spine. She stood very still in front of its gates, staring up at the tall building with its sheer walls and barred windows. Somehow, she hadn't imagined there would be barred windows, but the doors were barred, too, and there were iron spikes on top of the walls. From within, she could hear voices: some of them sounded like they were talking, but others cackled in a way that made hairs rise on the back of her neck. One was muttering something over and over. Ada was too far away to make out the words, but it had a strange, erratic rhythm to it that almost didn't sound human.

Ada took a deep breath, unwrapping her arms from around her chest, letting her hands fall to her sides and flexing her fingers a few times. If she had to go in there to find a decent dress, then so be it. She was going to be a governess and save her mother – no matter what it took.

*And maybe, when I'm a governess for a rich family, I'll find Quincy again.*

Ada pushed down the thought. This was for Mama. But still... it was a beautiful hope.

The doors of the mission house opened, and two people came out wearing a white uniform. They looked as though they had just finished work; talking, they headed toward the gates. Ada hurried forward.

"Excuse me," she called out as they reached the gates. "I'm sorry to trouble you, but I was wondering where you sell clothes to the poor here?"

The two women stopped. The taller one snorted, shaking her head. "We don't sell clothes here," she said angrily.

"But... but what about the clothes that people donate to you?"

"Those are for the inmates," said the taller one.

"Don't you know what this mission house is, girl?" demanded the other.

They turned and hurried off, leaving Ada none the wiser. *Inmates.* Was this some kind of a prison? But no one donated clothes to a prison. It had to be something like a workhouse, Ada decided, turning to look up at it.

As she did so, she saw the iron gate swinging slowly shut. Before it could close completely, Ada lunged forward, grabbing the cold bars. It was heavy, but she managed to keep it open just a crack – just enough to keep it from locking.

She froze, staring up at the huge building. What next? There seemed to be only one option. No one was outside in the bleak, empty courtyard; it was a straight dash to the door, and it seemed as though the two women had been just as careless with the door as they had been with the gate. Ada could see a chink of light around the edge of it.

She took a deep breath and pulled the gate open with a long, squealing sound. Slipping through the gap, she left the gate, dashed across the courtyard, skipped up the steps and grasped the door. It opened easily at her touch, and she ducked inside.

She was standing in a long, narrow hallway, all grey walls with no windows, scrubbed absolutely clean of any kind of dirt or emotion. It felt almost as though no one had ever been inside this place before, as though no one had ever contaminated it with anything messy or nonsensical or human.

The feeling was intimidating. Ada swallowed hard, then began to shuffle forward. Should she call out? But people might chase her away; they usually did. She would have to find the place where they stored the clothes on her own, wherever that might be.

Doubts crept through her mind, whispering in her ears as she moved along the hallway. What if she hadn't heard Sophia correctly and no one donated clothes to the mission house after all? What if there weren't any clothes in here, and she was wasting her time completely? But it was the only chance Ada could see for herself, so she kept moving, her heart pounding in her throat.

A voice made her jump. She cowered back against the wall, but the voice was muffled, as though it was coming from another room. It repeated the same words over and over.

"Only Kidderminster carpet will do," a man's voice was yammering. "Only Kidderminster carpet will do." He giggled then, a frightening chuckle that made Ada's hair stand on end.

"Yes, yes," muttered an impatient voice. "Kidderminster carpet, I know, I know. Now hold still."

"Only Kidderminster carpet will do."

There was a sloshing sound, like water in a basin. "Now try to keep your sheets clean," said the impatient voice.

"Only Kidderminster..."

The door slammed. "He's such a bore," complained the impatient voice.

"I know. I can barely stand to listen to him," said another voice.

"And look at these trousers. They're utterly ruined. Soiled to death. I say — I don't think I can take it here much longer. All these lunatics are going to drive me quite mad, too."

"Don't say that." The second voice shuddered. "Imagine going mad and ending up in here."

"Well." The first voice cleared its throat. "Here, give me those things. I'll put them in the laundry."

Footsteps approached, and Ada froze. Should she leave this place, and flee? This couldn't be where Sophia had sent her gowns. She must have misunderstood. But she heard the slam of the front door and knew she was trapped. Desperate, her heart pounding, she rushed forward, taking the first right turn she saw to avoid both sets of footsteps and bolting down the hallway.

"Hey," shouted the impatient voice. "What's that noise?"

A door appeared to Ada's left. She grabbed it and flung herself inside, closing the door silently behind her. She was inside a small, dank, windowless room; her eyes had not yet adjusted to the interior, but she could feel the shape of shelves around her. A storeroom. Blundering forward, she tripped over some boxes. Bottles fell to the ground, rattling on the floor.

"I heard something in here," someone called outside.

Ada's fingers found something – a box – a big, empty box. She scrambled inside, her eyes just picking out an empty sack in the gloom. Seizing it, she pulled it over the box and lay curled inside, her legs pressed up against one side, her back against the other. She had to tuck her chin right into her chest, and it made her neck ache at once.

The door creaked, the inside of the room brightening.

"Who's there?" shouted the impatient voice. "Mavis? Have you been wandering about again?"

Ada held her breath, not daring to move. The only part of her in motion seemed to be her heart, which beat a wild, thundering tattoo against her chest, loud as the hoofbeats of morning traffic. There was a quiet footstep, someone coming into the room. Ada squeezed her eyes tight shut. Her heart... they must have heard the wild rhythm of her heart.

"What is it, Roland?" asked the second voice.

The footsteps stopped. "I think Mavis has gotten out again. She must be hiding in here."

"Oh, no. Don't worry," said the second voice. "Mavis is snug as a bug in her cell – I just paused to check in on her when I came past."

"All right, then. Must have been my imagination," said Roland.

"Don't say that."

The door closed, and Ada knew a tiny second of relief before she heard it: the clink of a bolt sliding home.

"No, no, no, no," she whispered under her breath, shoving aside the sack and scrambling out of the box. She scrambled over to the door and grabbed for it, careful not to twist the knob, but applying her eye to the crack. It was as she had feared. The door had been bolted from the outside.

Dismay turned Ada's limbs to water. She folded to the ground, cupping a hand over her nose and mouth to muffle her sobs of terror. This was no haven where she could find clothes to make her into a governess. This was a prison – an insane asylum, populated by the mentally ill, a place of madness and cruelty. And now she was trapped in here, trapped like a bird in a small room, beating herself against the glass again and again and again.

# CHAPTER 10

THERE WERE TIMES, as the long and dark and lonely hours slipped by, that Ada considered screaming for help. With every hour that passed, the thought grew more and more attractive. Her aching head leaning back against the wall, her legs crossed on the cold and unforgiving floor, Ada tried to imagine that course of action turning out well. If she screamed for help, maybe one of the orderlies would come. Not Roland, the impatient one – but the other, gentler one. Maybe he would be kind and sympathetic and tell her it was all just a misunderstanding and take her nicely outside into the sun and let her go...

She let out a quiet, derisive snort at her own daydream. Of course, things wouldn't go that way. They never did. They would think she was a thief breaking into the asylum, and she would be taken to the police... and then? Imprisoned?

Hanged, perhaps. It was difficult to tell; anything could happen if you were a scruffy-looking girl with no one on your side.

She tried not to think about Mama. What Mama would do when Ada wasn't home tonight — and it had to be night now; the asylum had fallen into an eerie silence but for the odd burst of jabbering, a cackle here and there, sometimes a distant cry that could have been the call of some night bird or a terrible scream. In the dark and lonely storeroom, Ada couldn't tell. She didn't sleep. Thirst sucked the back of her throat as dry as though she'd stuffed her mouth with sawdust, but she dared not touch a thing inside that storeroom. If she really did steal anything, she knew she was done for. The thirst spread over her tongue, making her mouth feel like it was made from sandpaper. Every time she swallowed, she could feel dryness on dryness, and it made her gag.

Some fevered doze must have come over her at some point in the night, because suddenly there were footsteps coming toward her and someone was speaking. It was Roland, the impatient orderly, and he was right outside the door.

Ada gasped, scrambling to her feet as quietly as she could. She rushed to the box, seized it, then hesitated. Should she try to hide or escape? Her thirst pleaded her to flee.

"... some more flour for breakfast," Roland was grumbling. "That's hardly my job then, is it? I tells the cook, you go fetch it yourself. But Matron heard that, and she wasn't a bit happy."

"She's still angry about Kidderminster's trousers, too," said the second voice.

"Oh, I know that," said Roland bitterly. "But what am I to do about some madman who soils his trousers?"

The lock clicked, and she knew the door was about to open, letting in delicious light and air and freedom. Her mind was instantly made up. When the door opened, she would flee. If she could just hide behind the door, and if the orderlies would just come all the way into the room, she could do it.

Holding her breath, she stood against the wall where she would be hidden when the door opened. Her shoulders squeezed against the shelves. She didn't move as the hinges creaked and the door swung slowly open.

"Hey," said Roland suddenly, "something seems different in here."

Ada's thudding heart seemed to judder to a halt.

"Different?" said Hubert. "What do you mean?"

"I don't know... emptier." Roland paused. "Was there anything in that box yesterday?"

Ada squeezed her eyes shut, biting down on her lip, praying that they wouldn't look around. Roland had moved into her vision now; he was a stout man with messy brown hair.

"No, nothing," supplied Hubert. He appeared beside Roland, both of them with their backs to Ada. Hubert was lanky, with long, unkempt blond hair. "I unpacked some tins of beans from it yesterday and forgot to take it away."

Ada's shoulders released a tiny bit of tension, and she realized then that this was the perfect time to run. Neither of them thought she was there. All she needed was to grab the door, dodge around it, and bolt – and hope that the front door was wide open...

*One door at a time.* Ada sucked in a deep breath, summoned every scrap of courage she had, and flung herself forward.

Her arm slammed painfully along the doorknob as she seized the door, her balance teetering, scrambling to get around it. There was a yell from Hubert; one of them wheeled around, fingers brushing angrily across the back of her neck as though to grab her by the scruff like a stray dog. But somehow no one caught hold of her; somehow, she was in the doorway looking down the blissfully open, clean sweep of hallway, and she was free –

"Got you," roared Roland.

A fist closed on her wrist like a shackle, jerking her back so hard that something wrenched painfully in her shoulder. Ada shrieked, spinning around from the momentum of it, and looked momentarily into a pair of cold grey eyes. They widened.

"Wait," Roland said. "I don't know you."

Ada took advantage of his momentary indecision. She flung up her knee, slamming into his belly, and he let out a yelp of pain. His fingers loosened on her arm. Throwing herself back, Ada wrenched out of his grip, whirled around, and ran head-long into Hubert. Tall though he was, he was unyielding, and he threw a skinny pair of arms around her and lifted her clean off the floor.

"Let me go," Ada shrieked, her voice as high and piercing as a bird's cry. "Let me go. I'm not mad. I'm not mad."

"Grab her legs," Hubert barked.

Hard hands locked around Ada's ankles.

"NO. No," Ada screamed. "I'm not mad. Let me go."

But she was so frightened, and her screams were so high-pitched, that she might as well have been mad; mad with fear and panic as these unknown men bore her forth to what may just as well be her doom. She flailed, but their grip on her was immovable.

"In here," panted Roland.

A door squeaked, and Ada was dragged into a terrifyingly silent, cold, and plain room. There was one tiny window, very high up, very much covered in iron bars. No wardrobe, no trunk, nothing. The cord for the gas light was on the outside; the light itself was a simple, naked thing cowering against a back corner. A narrow cot was pushed up against the opposite wall. There were thick, leather straps on it, with great buckles, and they were stretched and wrinkled as though some hapless soul had strained and strained against them. Everything reeked of urine, and Ada noticed a chamber pot in the corner.

The sight of the room, and the prospect of being trapped in here, made everything inside her turn cold. She froze in Hubert's arms, her mind racing with terror. She knew there was no way of getting out of here. With the sinking sensation of being sucked into some great, cold bog, Ada was suddenly and completely certain that she was going to be stuck inside this room with this tiny window and this awful smell.

But ... if she was careful, she might escape – later.

She forced herself to take a long, deep breath, somehow succeeding, as they bore her toward the bed, and went completely limp. Even though it felt like the most foolishly vulnerable thing in the world, she closed her eyes and allowed her head to loll back, forcing every muscle in her body to relax.

"Is she dead?" asked Roland, with vague interest.

"No, I can feel her heart," said Hubert. "Tired herself out with all of her struggling, more likely."

They heaved her onto the cot; Ada forced herself to stay limp even though her head bounced painfully on the hard straw mattress.

"Does she look familiar to you... at all?" Roland asked nervously.

"No. But there are so many in here..." Hubert trailed off.

"I know." Roland swallowed. "And do you know, she must have been hiding in that storeroom all night. I thought it was Mavis, but it must have been her."

"You're right," said Hubert. His voice quavered. "Matron isn't going to be happy."

There was a long, dreadful silence – so long that Ada considered leaping to her feet and bolting for the door right there and then.

"Well," said Roland, slowly, "maybe Matron doesn't need to know."

There was a brief, pregnant pause. Then the two men shuffled out, and Ada heard the door close behind them.

As soon as she was sure they were gone, Ada jumped to her feet. The door had a very small window in it – also covered with an iron grille – but at least Ada could see a little way down the corridor each way if she stood on tiptoe to peer through it. She supposed that this window was for the people outside to check on the asylum's inmates.

It seemed that this mysterious Matron, whoever she was, would not be at all amused if Hubert and Roland managed to lose a patient. Ada needed to get the two men to panic. She knew from her many escapes on the street that a panicking man made bad decisions, and that she might be able to get away from them, if she could get them to panic a little.

There was only one thing she could think of doing. She assumed the inmates here must get meals and water sometimes. If she could make them think she wasn't here, she might be able to get them to panic enough to run out into the hallway – maybe leaving the door open.

Her throat ached with thirst, and for a moment, she considered staying here just a little while. Just until nightfall, or whenever it was that the inmates here were given anything to eat or drink. But the thought of poor Mama, who had spent a whole night in the tenement on her own, who might not even have had a penny left for supper last night, drove her on.

She rolled onto her side, slipping out of the bed. It was small and narrow, but there was some space underneath it – space enough to hide, thanks to the sheets that hung over the flat, inadequate mattress. There were cobwebs underneath it, and balls of dust, and a faintly pungent odour that made Ada gag a little. She didn't want to think about what else might be under there. Taking a deep breath, she flattened herself to the disgusting floor and slid into the darkness underneath the bed.

Now she just had to hope that her desperate plan would succeed.

# CHAPTER 11

"*WHAT?*"

"I said, she's not there."

The strident voices jerked Ada from her cramped half-slumber under the bed. Her eyes snapped open, and she tensed, glancing at what little she could see of the door from her position under the mattress. It was still closed.

"How can she not be there?" Roland demanded angrily.

"I don't know, but she isn't." Hubert retorted.

"Matron's going to kill us," Roland hissed.

The doorknob rattled. "It's still locked," said Hubert uncertainly. "Maybe she's in there."

"In *where*, Hubert?" yelled Roland. "Look at the room. She's gone – and you and I are as good as dismissed from this job."

Their voices rose, and Ada allowed herself a tiny smile of satisfaction, even though her throat felt raw and swollen with thirst. The orderlies were panicking. She might just be able to get out of this room...

*And then what?*

The door banged open, and the two orderlies rushed inside. Ada cowered against the floor, her worries for the future forgotten in her terror over the present.

"She's got to be here somewhere." A pair of large boots appeared right in front of Ada's face, between her and the tantalizing gap of the open door. Clearly, they thought the bed too low to the floor to accommodate anyone hiding there.

"She's not. You know she's not," said Hubert. "Roland, what are we going to do? I've got a wife... children... I have to feed them."

"You didn't manage to get Matron to tell you who she was?"

"No. No luck. She doesn't even know anyone escaped last night." Hubert moaned. "Imagine what she'll do when she finds out that someone escaped from the whole asylum."

"Not necessarily," said Roland slowly. "We... we could tell her that an impostor came in. Someone posing to be the girl's brother, or husband, or father. We'll forge his signature in the book. Say that he came to take her away."

"That could work." Hubert took an eager step forward toward Roland. "That could save us both."

Ada tried not to think about the children that Hubert had mentioned. She had to think of Mama, and freedom. And in taking that step forward, Hubert had opened the way for her to escape. Ada took a deep breath, ignored the cramping in her limbs, and threw herself forward.

It was a mad scramble to get out from under the bed. Roland's shout echoed through the room, a whip to Ada's back despite the stiffness that made her joints feel filled with sand. Limbs screaming with pain, Ada still bolted, her blood pulsing with urgency, the doorway beckoning. Her hand found the door-knob and she flung herself into the hallway with a desperate cry of panic and triumph. In a moment of terrified inspiration, she yanked the door shut behind her and slammed the bolt closer.

"Hey. HEY," roared Roland, slamming both hands against the door so that it shuddered. But the iron bolt did not budge.

Ada did not look back at them. She just ran, blind and panicking, a rabbit fleeing into an unfathomable warren. Trying to guess madly at which hallways she'd taken coming in, she found herself running in and out and up and down, stairs appearing before her, bolting down them, always with the sound of footsteps ringing in her ears, always unable to discern whether they were her own or some pursuer's. But there were shouts behind her, and there must be many orderlies in this place. They'd be chasing her. They'd find her.

She crashed through a tall wooden door that banged deafeningly back on its hinges, and she was in a vast kitchen that reeked of gruel and cabbage. Even that foul smell made her belly cry out for food. Steam clouded the air, and several wide-eyed young faces were turned toward her, staring.

Servants. She had to be near the servants' entrance.

She bolted through the kitchen. Thinking her some dangerous lunatic, the cooks and maids leaped back, screaming in panic. Ada took the blessing as it came. She rushed forward, crashing through the tables, dodging hard in front of what turned out to be an oven, but she couldn't turn in time and threw out a hand against the corner of the oven. Blazing pain seared across her palm.

The pain gave her a jolt of frightening strength just as the voices yelled from behind her. "There she goes. Stop her. Stop her."

Panic surged in her chest. Ada's eyes picked out the crack of the door in the gloom. A tiny scullery-maid was just going out of the door, carrying a huge rubbish bin. It was rather too big for her to carry, and she turned slowly, cumbersomely.

Ada ran toward her, throwing herself forward with a despairing cry. The little maid let out a shriek of horror and dropped the bin, which fell across the doorway. Ada took a wild, hopeless leap. Her feet caught on the back corner of the bin, and she fell, palms and chin first, skidding painfully down the back stairs, blood in her mouth, her burned hand searing with pain, and the wall right in front of her.

"Get her," shrieked Hubert's high-pitched voice.

The wall. The wall with the iron spikes on top. But Ada would rather face iron spikes a thousand times than a single second more in that awful, awful room. Her eyes found the back wall of what had to be the stables, a wheelbarrow standing beside it. If she could find the strength...

Fear gave her that strength. She was on her feet somehow and running toward the wheelbarrow as she heard the bin being thrust out of the way, her pursuers right on her heels. Her right foot found the wheelbarrow and launched her, despairingly, toward the roof of the stable. Her fingers dug into dusty thatch, and somehow, she was pulling herself up, running over the stable wall. It gave painfully under her left foot, and she tumbled headlong, her ankle burning, but she was rolling to her feet, her pursuers were all too heavy for the wall, they were shouting along below her, and she was going to make it. She leaped for the wall and seized one of the spikes. It was just sharp enough to dig painfully into her wounded hand; she let it go, fell back with a scream of pain, and Hubert's hand closed around her ankle.

"I've got her," he shouted.

Ada kicked out before she could think what she was doing. There was a nasty, meaty sound as her heel met Hubert's face, and he fell back with a cry. There was no time for regret. She was on her feet and launching toward the wall again, grabbing the spine with her good hand now, and it dug into her skin, but she was already scrabbling up onto it and over the spikes. And beyond the wall, blessedly, there was another stable – and a muck heap.

Ada took a flying leap. Her feet sank into the squishy mess of straw and manure, and she tumbled forward, hands, head, back, the filthy mess skidding up her skirts and queasily onto her skin. But she was free, and her feet found cobbles. She dodged between the stables and out into the street, and the shouts were already fading behind her as she disappeared into the busy afternoon crowd.

Her throat was burning, her body was aching, and she was hungrier than she'd ever been in her life. But she'd escaped that awful, awful place.

For now, that would have to be enough.

Quincy's heart fluttered in his chest. Maybe, just maybe...

He pushed through the crowd, looking this way and that, both searching and checking that he wasn't being followed. It had been hard enough to slip away from his governess when they were waiting at the tailor's. Quincy hated the tailor's, even though he was being forced to go there more and more often now that he was old enough to meet "important people". He hated being measured for suits he didn't want to wear in order to attend gatherings he didn't want to go to, all in order to speak to people he didn't like. Everything else about learning about Papa's shipping business was just fine. Quincy liked learning about the oceans, the products, the different countries. Even the arithmetic was all right.

But the insufferable bigwigs with their patronizing voices and their cold, empty eyes, and clammy handshakes – he could understand now why Mama had hated all of it.

As always, a swift pang of perfect agony ran through him at the thought of Mama. It was so powerful that he felt his feet stutter on the pavement as he passed by the bakery. *Oh, Mama...* If only she'd never left him. Everything had gone wrong then.

Quincy stopped, sighing. He was right opposite the bakery now, very near to where he'd last seen her... or thought he'd seen her.

Slowly, he turned, searching up and down the street with his eyes. It was difficult to imagine what Ada would look like now. Beautiful, he imagined. She'd been beautiful even two years ago, when they were both still so little, when he hardly knew what beauty even was. But he knew now, and when he'd seen her... It had been like being faced with an angel, albeit an angel in rags, an angel with a pinched, pale face and hollow cheeks.

His heart burned. Could it really be that Ada, his Ada, was so thin and sad and ragged? Mama would have hated to see her like this. Had Ada really been begging? What would he do if he found her? He closed his eyes in pain, remembering that day. The driving rain. The moment when their eyes had locked, and his leaping joy when he'd been certain, absolutely certain that he was looking at his only friend in all the world. He had wanted to run to her. She had started toward him, as though to run to him, too. But when Papa had called out, Quincy had known that he would only hurt Ada if he ever saw her again... and he'd shaken his head, told her to stop, walked away from her life.

He groaned with mental agony. Even if he found Ada again, he didn't know how to help her. Not with Papa looking over his shoulder, making sure of his every movement, despising his every softness, striving to stamp out every spark of kindness and compassion that Mama had worked to plant in his young heart.

It was all irrelevant, he supposed. She wasn't here.

All the times he'd come here to look, she hadn't been here.

# PART III

# CHAPTER 12

*Two Years Later*

ADA SET down the huge stack of plates, pausing to roll her head back on her shoulders, trying to ease the constant ache in her neck and shoulders. She took a deep breath, shaking out her aching hands, and gazed with dismay at the stacks and stacks of plates and glasses, knives and forks, spoons and cups waiting for her on the enormous table beside the sink.

It was incredible just how many dirty dishes could be generated by the patrons of this fairly small hotel. Fairly small, Ada supposed, because one single unlucky girl could be employed to wash them all. It was all she did: she cleared the table after breakfast, washed the dishes; by then it was time to clear the table after lunch, and wash those dishes. Then supper... and more dishes. To say nothing of tea and cakes and elevenses and all the other things that the well-to-do guests of the hotel wanted.

She paused for a moment longer to stretch out a cramp in her right shoulder, and a harsh voice fell across her shoulders like the crack of a whip. "You. Carter. Get back to work."

Ada jumped, nervousness instantly knotting in the pit of her belly. "Yes, Miss Allan. Right away, Miss Allan."

The head housekeeper was an imposing stone tower of a woman, the buttresses of her cheeks and jaw supporting two eyes that blazed out at Ada like a fiery cauldron of burning oil, waiting to be poured on whichever hapless attacker dared to approach her walls. Her mouth was flat and solid, an arrow slit. She launched another insult from it. "Lazy scum. That can't be all of the dishes. Bring the last of them and wash them immediately."

"Yes, Miss Allan," said Ada quickly.

She turned and scurried away from the kitchen toward the dining hall. It was no surprise that Miss Allan had never married; Ada didn't think even the most charming of princes could dare to breach her defences.

Smoothing down her little white apron, Ada tried to slip unobtrusively into the dining hall. It was mostly empty, but often a few knots of late diners would stay behind, perhaps nodding to sleep over the last few sips of a glass of wine too many or just enjoying the company of friends. Tonight, however, Ada knew that most of the patrons had gone off to the opera. There was only one old woman sitting contentedly at a table near the back, her dirty plate still in front of her, sipping slowly at the last of a glass of red wine.

Ada hovered nervously by her elbow. Nothing angered a wealthy patron like a waitress who took their cup too early, except a waitress who took their cup too late. It was impossible to get it right, and when the patrons were unhappy, they complained to the owner, and when the owner was unhappy, he told Miss Allan, who beat the maids. Ada's back was still bruised and sore from the last beating. She didn't want to go through that again.

Taking the last sip of her wine, the old woman looked up at her. She was strikingly pretty, not despite her age, but because of it; the folds of her wrinkled face only made her blue eyes seem brighter, and the shimmer of her long white hair seemed to ooze purity and wisdom.

"You've been up and down those steps a hundred times tonight, my girl," she said.

Ada hesitated, nervousness rising in her throat. "I beg your pardon, ma'am?" She was acutely conscious of angry Miss Allan waiting for her back in the kitchen and now confused that this woman had even looked her in the eye, let alone actually addressed her.

"You must be tired." The old woman smiled at her but didn't surrender the wineglass. "I'm here regularly, you know, and you've been a wonderful little waitress."

"Thank you, ma'am," said Ada uncertainly.

The old woman sighed and finally held out the wineglass. "Well, I'm off to bed. Have a nice evening, young lady."

"Thank you, ma'am." A rush of relief ran through Ada as she took the glass.

She turned to scurry away, but as she did so, she heard the scrape of the old woman's chair as she rose. Then a sudden gasp, a yelp of dismay, and a splintering crash. Ada spun around just in time to see the old woman fall. Her ankle was awkwardly twisted around a chair leg; as she fell, she had grabbed at the tablecloth, pulling it toward her. A vase of flowers lay shattered on the floor, water and petals every-where – and the old woman was falling straight toward it.

"Ma'am," Ada cried, lunging forward.

Dropping the wineglass on the table, she grabbed for the old woman's arm. It was too late to stop her from falling. Instead, the old woman turned as she fell, landing heavily on her hip and elbow, her head falling straight toward the leg of the table. Ada dived to stop it, grabbing the old woman's head just in time. Her knuckles rapped painfully against the table. The old woman grabbed at her dress with a desperate claw, crying out in pain and fright.

"Oh – oh," she cried. "My hand."

She raised it, blood coursing down her wrist from a cut on her palm. There was a bloodied, jagged piece of glass lying on the floor beside her.

Ada grabbed a clean napkin from the table and pressed it over the old woman's hand. "Help," she called out, glancing around. "Help!"

To her relief, it wasn't Mrs. Allan who came running, but a well-dressed gentleman she vaguely recognized as being one of the guests. The old woman's son-in-law, she thought.

"Oh, Beatrice," he said. "What happened?" He crouched down beside her, hardly sparing Ada a second glance.

"I tripped over the chair leg, dear," said Beatrice shakily. "I was just enjoying the last of my wine..."

"Maybe a little too much wine, eh?" said the son-in-law.

"Thomas." Beatrice managed a weak chuckle.

"Let's get you to a doctor. Did you hurt your head?" Thomas asked.

Beatrice looked up at Ada.

"No," she said. "Thanks to this lovely young lady." She grabbed Ada's arm with her good hand. "You did me a great kindness, young lady, and likely saved me from causing myself far greater harm than a silly cut."

Ada didn't know what to say, so she just gave Beatrice a wobbling smile.

"What's your name, dear?" Beatrice asked.

"Beatrice, is this really the time?" asked Thomas, who was helping the old woman to her feet. "I really think you should see a doctor about your hand."

"Yes, yes, dear, but let me just find out this nice young lady's name," said Beatrice.

"Ada." Ada cleared her throat. "Ada Carter."

"Well, Miss Ada Carter, I owe you a debt of gratitude," said Beatrice. "I'll be sure to tell the proprietor all about you."

"*After* you've been to the doctor," insisted Thomas. "Come now." He took Beatrice's hand from Ada, keeping the napkin firmly pressed over her palm. "Let's go."

Ada watched them go, feeling a curious little spark of warmth at the old woman's obvious kindness, even before Ada had helped her. The warmth was quickly replaced by a sucking sense of dread.

"ADA!" thundered Miss Allan's voice from the kitchen. "Where are you, you lazy wretch?"

Ada sighed, picking up the last stack of dishes. Now she would have to wash the floors, too, and explain to Miss Allan what had happened to the napkin.

If Beatrice could only confirm that Ada hadn't stolen or damaged that napkin, that would be more kindness than she expected from anyone.

❦

MAMA'S COUGHS tore through the steady undercurrent of background noise that always filled the air in this dingy, reeking tenement. It was an even worse tenement than the one they had lived in when Mama had first gotten the job cleaning fish at the docks. When Ada's begging had become less and less productive, they'd been forced to move nearer the docks, hoping for Ada to find a similar job to Mama's. The rent was cheaper here, too. But that was with good reason.

The entire building rattled as another train passed right by it, carrying cargo that had crossed the oceans out to the rest of England. Ada wondered what that train would contain as she huddled over the stub of candle that cast a pathetic half-circle of insufficient light on her corner of the sleeping pallet. Ivory? Tea? Spices? Expensive things that only the rich could afford. Well, apart from the tea. And the way things stood now, tea was rapidly becoming yet another thing sucked out of Ada's life by the constant, ever-growing bog of poverty.

Around her, the sounds of the tenement building rose and fell. Ada and Mama lived in the attic, squashed against the ceiling that was cold in winter and hot in summer. Below them, Ada could hear the drunken carousing of sailors in the alehouse on the ground floor. There were shrieks and giggles, too, from the hopeless women and hollow-eyed ladies of the night that the sailors loved to bring home. Snores, thick and drunken things, emanated from other sailors' rooms.

Compared with the constant cacophony of noise coming from all around them, Mama's coughs were a quiet sound. But they shook Ada's world, cutting painfully through the background hum of their poverty.

"Mama?" she murmured softly, turning away from the precious candle stub to put a hand on her mother's shoulder. "Are you all right?"

"Mmm," Mama mumbled, sounding half-asleep.

Ada sat still for a few moments, listening to Mama's breathing. It deepened gradually and peacefully into sleep, but there was still a dread rattle somewhere in her chest that Ada didn't like at all. She twisted in her spot on the sleeping pallet and tucked a little more of the thin blanket around her mother, trying not to care that this exposed her knees to the cold.

"Oh, Mama," she murmured. "I'm going to get you out of this – I really am."

Mama didn't stir; she was fast asleep, and Ada knew that even if she'd been awake, she wouldn't have paid much attention to Ada's words. If she was in a good mood, she might have said, "Yes, dear", but Mama was so seldom in a good mood these days. In fact, she was seldom in any kind of a mood. It was as though every part of her that could feel or be anything had been scooped out, leaving a hollow, Mama-shaped shell.

Ada missed her so much, even as she lay with her back pressed against her mother.

She gritted her teeth against the flow of tears that threatened to escape and run down her cheeks. Taking a few deep breaths to hold them back, she turned her attention back to the scrap of newspaper in her hands. It was a single article that she'd been able to tear out of the bit of greasy newspaper that Mama's boss had used to wrap up their half-rotten fish for the day. *Another British Defeat at Schuinshoogte*, it claimed in loud block capitals.

Ada's eyes struggled over and over to identify the sounds in that last word. *Schuinshoogte*. It sounded Dutch, but she knew that the war was in South Africa. Did that make any sense? Her mind had endured twelve hours of work that day and was struggling to eke out any meaning even from the English words she knew well.

She paused, raising a hand to her aching temples, and massaged them for a moment. The stub of candle guttered dangerously, as though it would go out at any second now. Ada forced her eyes open and focused on the newspaper again. She had to finish this article before the candle went out. She had promised herself that she would read a little every single night, to cling to the tiny piece of hope she had left: her education.

Otherwise, she would never be a governess, never able to get Mama out of this filthy tenement.

She tried not to lift her eyes from the paper. It was easier to believe that she might really be a governess someday if she kept reading, kept focused on what she was doing. Otherwise, she might look up, and look around, and see the hopelessness around her: the gaps in the building's walls stuffed with bits of newspaper; the chamber pot that served as their only bathroom; the distant shimmer of the Thames through the last glass pane left in the window, its filthy reek rising into the night air. There were days when she thought it would be easier to be like Mama, to let go of all this and just give up.

But she couldn't do that. She couldn't give up on Mama.

So she took a deep breath, squinted against the fading light, and kept fighting the darkness with each word that she read.

# CHAPTER 13

ADA STRAIGHTENED UP SLOWLY, one hand on the small of her back, stretching out her aching muscles as she paused in mopping the hallway floor. As she did so, she glanced around nervously for Miss Allan. Even this momentary pause in work could be cause for a tongue-lashing – or a real lashing – in the tyrannical housekeeper's eyes.

But Miss Allan wasn't watching right now, so Ada permitted herself a moment to close her eyes and lean on her mop, allowing the wave of utter exhaustion to wash over her. It had to be close to half past ten, and Ada still had to finish this mopping before she could start the half-hour walk home. She could only hope that Mama was able to buy something for supper with the money Ada had given her that morning. Lunch had been nearly twelve hours of hard work ago, and she was as hungry as she was tired.

She straightened, ignoring the stiff and steady ache in her muscles, and got back to mopping. It was brain-dead work, the mop going in circles, back and forth, automatic by now. There was something almost soothing about it, but her mind was crying out in desperation. She started playing with numbers in her head, giving herself simple mathematical problems to solve. It was the only way she could stay sane through the plod of manual work, even when she was exhausted like this.

*What is one hundred and fifteen times twenty-two?*

She struggled for the answer, each step coming to her sluggishly. Was she just tired, or was she busy forgetting her education – the one thing she had left? A pang of fear ran through her. What if she forgot the things she'd learned, and could never become a governess?

The fear was quickly replaced with an aching sense of resignation. She'd been trying to find her way to work as a governess for the past two years. Part of her wanted to just accept that it was never going to happen, and that hopeless squalor was her lot for the rest of her life – and Mama's.

"Ah, there she is." said a bright voice from the landing.

Ada jumped, spinning around, her mop gripped tightly in both hands. In her experience, a booming voice behind one was never a good thing. But this time, it was Beatrice, beaming from ear to ear as she bustled toward Ada.

"Here she is, my little saviour," she said.

Thomas and his pale slender wife, Letitia, were standing behind Beatrice. Thomas gave her a tight-lipped smile; Letitia didn't look her in the eye. Ada had served them both before, but they never spoke to her.

Beatrice had no such reservations. She swept over to Ada and grasped her hands, beaming at her. "This is the young lady who caught me when I fell, Letitia," she said. "I'm so glad to see you – Ada, isn't it?"

"Yes, ma'am," said Ada. She knew she should feel flattered by Beatrice's affections, but in reality, she wished the old woman would just go to her room and get to bed so that Ada could finish the mopping. All she wanted was to go home.

"Well, you did me a great service, young lady," said Beatrice. "And you've always been a lovely waitress, too." She waved at Letitia. "Don't just stand there, darling, give her the package."

Looking as though she would rather be anywhere except here, Letitia shuffled forward and held out a large parcel wrapped in brown paper and packing string. Beatrice took it. "Here. This is for you." She offered it to Ada.

Ada reached for it, then drew back. "You're very kind, ma'am, but I can't accept anything from guests. The housekeeper would be irate."

"Oh, nonsense," said Beatrice. "I'll talk to the housekeeper."

She tugged at the string, letting the parcel fall open.

"I know it's difficult to get good clothes in your situation, apart from one's uniform, and you're about the same shape as Letitia was at your age, and this was just rotting in the bottom of a wardrobe – I thought it would be perfect for you."

Ada's breath caught in her chest as the paper fell away, revealing a neatly folded dress lying in Beatrice's hands. It was more than just a sturdy dress that didn't seem to have holes in it, with fabric that wasn't so thin as to be transparent. It was a thing of beauty. She reached out slowly, letting her fingertips slide across the front. The colour was a rich emerald green, dark and solemn, and when she touched the fabric, it was thick and strong. She didn't think it could possibly have been worn more than a handful of times, it seemed that new.

"Ma'am," she breathed, staring up at Beatrice.

There was more than kindness in the old woman's eyes where they sparkled out at her from among a web of wrinkles. There was understanding, too, a spark of common suffering that passed briefly between them.

"It's yours, Ada," she said. "I'll go down to the kitchen and speak to the housekeeper myself. You take this and keep warm – and maybe find yourself a better position, too. From the way you speak, I can tell you've had some learning, haven't you? There's a lot that a clever young woman like you can do to better herself." She winked. "I should know."

"Oh, Mama, don't bring up the past," cried Letitia, as though the insinuation that her mother had once been poor was shameful to her.

"Why not? I promised myself I would never forget it, and I haven't," said Beatrice. "Here you are now, girl. Take it – and much as I have enjoyed your service, I hope not to see you in this position again at my next visit."

"Thank you," Ada stammered out, summoning the courage to reach out and grasp the dress in both hands. "Oh – thank you, thank you."

"Don't make a fuss, now. Wrap it up again before someone sees it," ordered Beatrice.

"Mother, please," sighed Letitia. "Can we go now?"

"We'll go to the kitchens first," said Beatrice firmly. "Come on."

She strode away, with Thomas and Letitia complaining in her wake. Ada stood frozen on the landing, staring down at the parcel, then up at the old woman's retreating back.

Suddenly she could feel that golden thread again, that pathway reopened, connecting her once again to the bright future she'd once had.

ALMOST, almost. Ada had mopped the floors, tidied the broom cupboard, put the things ready for setting the fires first thing tomorrow morning. All she had to do was put on her coat, then she could retrieve her parcel from where she'd tucked it away in the back of the broom cupboard and escape into the night.

She took small, quiet breaths, trying to act natural, as she took her coat from the nail by the kitchen door and shrugged it on. She would have to leave it unbuttoned if she wanted to tuck the parcel underneath her coat. Or would that only make Miss Allan more suspicious? Should she simply carry it normally and hope that the housekeeper would honour Beatrice's wishes?

Ada glanced nervously over her shoulder. Miss Allan was sitting by the kitchen table, a ledger open in front of her, writing down some kitchen records in large badly misspelled scrawl. Ada tried to ignore her annoyance at the sight of *Tomatos* and *Butermulk* and turned toward the broom cupboard, forcing herself to walk with casual indifference past the fireplace where the little scullery-maid was exhaustedly polishing the grate. Maybe Miss Allan wouldn't look up from where she was poring over the ledger.

Reaching into the cupboard, Ada fished her parcel out, clutching it tightly in both hands. She'd tied it up neatly again so that Miss Allan wouldn't see it. Tucking it under her arm, she turned to go, clearing her throat several times in a bid to make her voice more normal.

"Good night, Miss Allan," she said politely, the way she always did.

Miss Allan ignored her, the way she always did, and Ada crossed the kitchen toward the back door with trembling steps. She was nearly outside. She might make it without having to speak a single word to Miss Allan.

With every step she took, the weight of her responsibility hung on her shoulders as though an anchor had been chained to her. She knew that this dress represented her chances at a better future. But she had to be able to buy food right now, in the present, and if she wanted to do that, she had to keep her job at the hotel right up to the very minute that she found something better... that she became a governess. Twenty-five pounds a year. She could put Mama up in a nice cottage, or at least a better tenement, and neither of them would have to be hungry again...

Her hand was on the doorknob when Miss Allan spoke. "Did you think you could slip away from me with that, child?"

Ada froze, her heart racing. For a wild instant, she thought of simply throwing open the door and fleeing into the night. But the thought of Monday, just days away, rent day, stopped her in her tracks. Present, or future? How could she be forced to choose?

"Well?" Miss Allan barked. "Have you gone dumb as well as stupid?"

Ada took a few deep, trembling breaths. She turned around, keeping her eyes down, ignoring the little flare of anger in the centre of her chest.

"One of the guests gave this to me, ma'am," she said quietly, keeping the parcel clutched tightly under her arm. "She spoke to you about it. Didn't she?"

Miss Allan snorted. "Nosy old biddy. Thinking she can pry into my business downstairs when it's got nothing to do with her." She pushed back her chair, a bone-chilling scrape on the stone floor, and strode toward Ada. "Give me that."

Ada cringed backwards, clamping her arm down over her parcel and clutching it with her free hand.

"She just wanted to thank me for helping her," she said quietly. "Please, ma'am, she gave it to me."

"Thank *you*." Miss Allan barked out a laugh. "Why, if that poor old woman knew what a lazy little swine you are, and how I have to push and harry and chase you around to get you to do anything at all – well, she'd be giving *me* gifts, not you."

In the face of the exhaustion sucking at Ada's limbs, Miss Allan's words were a direct slap in the face. The housekeeper came to a halt in front of Ada, fixed her with a shimmering glare from beneath the crags of her eyebrows, and held out a monolithic hand. "Give it here," she ordered.

Ada swallowed hard. Should she submit? How else was she going to pay the rent? But something flared inside her at the ridiculous injustice of all this, and she found herself taking a step back, her grip tightening on the parcel.

"No," she said softly.

Miss Allan's eyes widened. They shimmered; molten rock building red-hot behind her eyes.

"I beg your pardon?" she hissed.

"This isn't yours, ma'am," said Ada, her voice trembling and quiet, but there was a force in it that frightened her. "It was given to me."

"Insolent cur," barked Miss Allan. She drew back a hand, and before Ada could react, it slapped agonizingly across her face – knuckles first. Pain bloomed over her nose and lips, and she took another staggering step back, bumping up against the door itself. Before she could move, Miss Allan was snatching at the parcel. "Give it here."

The scullery-maid squealed with shock.

"No," Ada cried, clutching at it, but she was stunned and sluggish from the blow and Miss Allan pulled hard. Paper ripped, and Ada was left clutching a wad of brown paper and string as Miss Allan lifted the dress out into the light. It fell open, glorious folds of strong wool, thick and elegant, its beautiful cut painting sleek lines against the gas light even though it was empty.

Ada felt a moment of wild hope. The dress was a pathetic thing against the monumental Miss Allan; a preposterous doll's dress clutched in her giant fingers. But Miss Allan let out a happy rumble. "Yes. This will fit my little niece a treat."

"Please," Ada said, straightening. Her body trembled uncontrollably. "Please... please give it back. I'm begging you, Miss Allan. I need it."

"What could a little maid like you need a beautiful thing like this for?" Miss Allan gave a harsh, barking laugh.

"Please, ma'am," Ada whimpered.

Miss Allan turned her back as though she hadn't heard. She tossed the dress carelessly onto the kitchen table, where it crumpled into a wrinkling heap. The dismissive gesture – as though she hadn't just thrown aside Ada's entire future – incensed something within her. She stepped forward, her fists clenched, a wave of sudden fury washing over her head.

"Give it back," she cried, reaching out and grasping Miss Allan's arm.

Miss Allan whirled around. Her arm slammed into Ada, sending her staggering back toward the door.

"Get out," she thundered. "How dare you lay hands on me."

"It's mine," Ada shouted.

"OUT!" roared Miss Allan. She took a frightening few steps toward Ada, her big hands bunched into fists. "I don't want to see you here again. GO!"

Ada's sob choked in her throat. She had lost them both, she realized with a wave of horror. Her present and her future were both in tatters.

"Miss Allan, please," she wailed.

Miss Allan reached past her, shoved the back door open, and seized Ada's arm in one of her giant hands. "You're dismissed," she barked. "Be gone."

She shoved Ada out into the cold night and slammed the back door with a resounding thud. Ada was left standing in the back courtyard, the icy breeze tracing its frigid fingers down her back, her heart pounding and pounding in her chest, alone.

# CHAPTER 14

ADA WASN'T sure how long she stood outside in that courtyard, motionless with shock and dismay. Just an hour ago, her heart had been filled with joy and excitement when Beatrice had given her that dress. For a few precious minutes, she had believed – really believed –things were going to get better, not just for her, but for poor, poor Mama.

It was the thought of Mama that jolted her out of her shock. She squeezed her eyes shut, trying to shut out the image of Mama's face when Ada would tell her what had happened. Mama would be appalled, and with good reason. Without Ada's wages from the hotel this week, they would have to make a horrifying decision: get thrown onto the streets or starve. They could have either a home or food; both was simply impossible.

Ada's breaths came in short, trembling gasps. Mama on the streets. It was unthinkable. The sound of Mama's coughs rippled through Ada's mind, and her heart quaked within her. She wouldn't last the winter on the streets. They would have to pay the rent, but what about food? How would they survive?

The answer was simple: they couldn't. Unless Ada had work, there was no way they could keep on living. The emerald green dress was glowing softly in the light of the kitchen's gas lamp: Ada could see it through the large kitchen window, lying on the table opposite Miss Allan as she bent over her ledger. It was only a few feet away from where Ada stood, but it might as well have been on the other side of the world.

Ada felt her hands bunch into fists. No. It *wasn't* on the other side of the world; it was right there in front of her, her ticket to a new life, and it was hers. Beatrice had given it to her, and Miss Allan had stolen it.

All that remained was to steal it right back.

She fed the fire inside her, imagining her mother in a clean little room, with enough food and a warm bed and a fireplace, with a window looking out onto a nice street or a tidy garden, Mama with roses in her cheeks again, maybe even a glimmer of the woman she used to be before Sophia died. The thought made that fire roar inside Ada's chest. Her key to giving her mother all of those things was lying there on the kitchen table, hers for the taking, and she was ready to take it.

Miss Allan had not locked the kitchen door. Why would she? To her mind, her word was law. But not to Ada Carter, not anymore.

Ada did not walk across to the door, she marched, arms swinging, teeth gritted, ready. She flung the door open in one ferocious movement.

Miss Allan looked up, the annoyance on her face quickly turning to shock. "What are you doing?" she roared.

The scullery-maid flew up from where she crouched by the gate, her hands black, and stared at Ada. "Ada, no. Get away from here," she cried.

Miss Allan was rising like a rupturing volcano, like an animated monolith come to furious life. "How dare you trespass in my kitchen," she thundered.

Ada didn't stop. She kept walking, her feet carrying her to the table, and reached for the dress. Miss Allan lunged for it at the same instant. Ada's fingers closed around the thick cloth of the skirt; Miss Allan had grabbed one of the sleeves.

"You won't take my future from me," Ada thundered. "Let go of the dress."

"Jonathan. JONATHAN," shrieked Miss Allan.

She was calling for the footman, who would be just in the servants' quarters down the hall, and Ada didn't have much time. She yanked at the dress but stopped when she heard the ping of popping seams.

"Let it go," Ada growled.

Miss Allan met her eyes, and with a sudden rush of both shock and power, Ada realized she saw fear in them. No one had ever stood up to Miss Allan like this before, Ada realized. She tightened her grip on the dress, leaning forward, fire blazing in her heart.

"I said, let it go," she shouted.

"Ada," cried the horrified scullery-maid.

Miss Allan didn't let go, but her hands wavered for an instant, and it was all Ada needed. She yanked at the dress, heard the rip of seams, and then it was free and she was stumbling backwards from the force of it, clutching the dress to her chest, and Jonathan was clumping into the kitchen, bleary-eyed in his nightclothes.

"Stop her. Stop her," roared Miss Allan.

Ada didn't hesitate. She had what she'd come for. Wheeling around, she bolted for the door.

"Stop her, Missy," roared Miss Allan.

The scullery-maid was hovering by the door, wide-eyed. When Ada rushed toward it, she hesitated for a trembling moment.

"Shut the door," shrieked Miss Allan.

The scullery-maid grabbed for the doorknob.

"No," cried Ada.

But instead of slamming the door, the maid pulled it wide open. "Go, Ada, run," she shouted.

Ada wanted to stop, to thank the little maid for what she'd done. There would be consequences, Ada knew; horrible consequences. But the door was wide, and the girl was waving her out, and she couldn't stop now, not for Mama's sake. So she bolted out into the cool evening, her future wadded up and clutched tightly in her arms, where no one could take it from her.

# CHAPTER 15

ADA WAS BREATHLESS, her legs cramping, as she hurried through the front door of the tenement building. The stench of it rose up, seeping into her lungs with each giant, sucking breath. Smoke, sweat, human excrement, mould, rotting food – it was a ripe and awful aroma, noxious and noisome, but it wasn't stopping her tonight. Nothing would stop her tonight.

"Mama," she called out, ignoring the spate of angry mutterings from the thin walls of the other tenement buildings at her midnight cries. "Mama, you won't believe what happened. It's just wonderful."

There was no answer, and Ada's heart hitched in her chest. She jogged down the makeshift hallway, heading for the back room. "Mama?" she cried, pulling aside the curtain that served as a door.

In the gloom of the tenement, she could barely make out the shape of her mother. There was no fire; the hearth was black and cold. The darkness felt absolute and impenetrable even though a tiny bit of light from the streetlamp outside was seeping in through the cracks in the walls and the bits of rags or paper they had used to stuff the larger holes in the boards covering the window. It seemed only to outline the darkness, to punctuate it, giving it form around the old wooden boxes that served as their furniture, the sleeping pallet in the corner, the lumpen, motionless form upon it.

Ada wanted to call to her mother, but the sound died on her lips. Surely... surely it couldn't be. The throbbing heat of her victory faded, blown out like a candle flame by the cold snuff of emptiness that seemed to ride from the room. It felt petty and silly now. The dress in her arms felt as insubstantial as an old newspaper.

There was a chill in the room that seeped into her bones, into her heart.

*Please... please... no.* Ada could place no coherence on her dread. Somehow, she shuffled forward, her breaths harsh and erratic. The dress fell to the floor from her numb fingers as she crouched down beside the sleeping pallet. She could just see Mama's form now, stretched out on her side, her head pillowed on her hands. Her face very smooth, very motion-less, very pale.

Almost peaceful.

Ada raised a hand that felt as though it was made from lead and settled it onto her mother's shoulder.

"Mama?" she breathed.

Mama rolled over, her eyes snapping open, the movement so quick and unexpected that Ada nearly screamed in shock.

"Oh," she cried, her surprise and fright swamped with relief. "Oh, Mama, Mama." She threw her arms around her mother, burying her face in Mama's neck and clinging to her, sobs rushing through her as the horrible fears subsided.

"Ada, don't make such a fuss," Mama croaked, her voice a hoarse ghost of what it once had been. "Come now. Stop that."

With difficulty, Ada swallowed her tears and sat up, wiping them away. She slowly began to take in her mother's appearance: the reddened eyes, the ashen cheeks, the way her chest moved in tiny, shallow gasps.

"Mama, what's the matter?" Ada asked, her body feeling cold with fear.

"I..." Mama closed her eyes. "I'm sorry."

Ada stared at her. She hadn't heard words like that from her mother in a long time. It was almost as though Mama had forgotten that Ada was a person at all; or, worse, that she was a person herself.

"I didn't go to work today, Ada," Mama whispered. "I couldn't. I'm just..." She raised a hand, as though to explain, then let it fall back onto the bed.

Ada reached out and pressed the back of her cold hand to Mama's forehead. It was blazing to the touch. Fear leaped in her heart as she realized the stakes. Mama would have lost her job; that much was certain. There was no room for illness in the dockworker's heartless life. Ada, too, had no work anymore, and the money that they'd earned for the week would be all gone. They had a few pennies for food, but the rent was due on Monday, and they would never make it.

"You have to leave me, child," Mama said softly.

Ada stared down at her. "What?"

Mama closed her eyes, as though keeping them open was just too much effort.

"Leave me. I'm done for," she whispered. "Go and live in the servants' quarters of the hotel – the owners will like that better, in any case. Make something of yourself." Her feeble hand flapped on the thin blanket; Ada took it, and Mama gripped it with more strength than she'd shown in years. "I'll only be a burden to you now."

"Mama, that's preposterous," said Ada. "I will never leave you."

Mama's eyes opened, shimmering with tears. "You can't care for both of us."

"I can if I become a governess."

Mama looked away. "Ada..."

"No, Mama. Listen to me." Ada rose, grabbing the dress from where she'd left it on the floor. "Look. One of the guests gave me this. I have a chance now, Mama, a real chance."

Mama stared at her, at the dress, which Ada held up in front of her. Sudden tears glimmered in Mama's eyes. "My precious child," she whispered. "You're so grown up."

"It could work," said Ada.

"It could." Mama struggled to sit up; Ada laid the dress aside on an old box and took Mama's arm, helping her to sit up with her back to the wall. "It looks like a tolerable fit, too. But there's a rip – there, on the bodice."

"I see," said Ada. She couldn't tell Mama where it had come from. "Maybe I can cover it up with my coat."

"No, no. You'll have to sew it." Mama struggled to sit a little straighter.

"I can't sew, Mama."

"And my hands are too weary. But I'll help you." There was a flash in Mama's eyes, a little of her old strength returning. "There's a stub of candle still, and a few matches. We'll pick the seams out of the hem of your old dress; it's not the right colour, but it'll do. And there's a bit of old wire on that board holding the window closed – we can make that into a needle."

Ada stared at her mother, joy thundering in her heart. She hadn't seen so much life in Mama for a long, long time. "Do you think we can do it?" she asked breathily.

Mama forced a wobbling smile.

"I... I don't care what happens to me, Ada," she said. "I'm tired. There's little left for me in this life. But you – you have a future." She held out a hand.

Ada gripped Mama's hand, hope flaring in her. This long night was about to get even longer, but at least she was no longer so alone.

She lit the candle, struggling with the damp matches, and then huddled on the sleeping pallet with the dress on her lap as Mama told her what to do. Each stitch took forever with the makeshift needle; the thread kept on slipping off it, and Ada struggled to see, her eyes aching from the strain of peering down through the flickering, inadequate light.

It was dawn by the time the rip was repaired; a thin, watery dawn, the day stumbling drunkenly onstage as an afterthought. But it was a dawn of terror and hope for Ada.

Mama's eyes were red and glazed as Ada held up the dress for the last time. "There," she whispered. "How does it look?"

"Perfect." Mama gave a wobbling smile.

Ada knew it looked far from perfect. The thread had broken many times as she'd struggled to sew, and the resultant seam was a messy, knotty thing. But it would do. It would have to do. It was the best that Ada had.

"I'm so tired," Mama whispered.

Ada set down the dress and helped Mama to lie back down, pulling the blanket over her. "I'm going to make you some broth with the two turnips we have left," she said quietly. "And then I'll go and find work."

If Mama had thought Ada still had her work at the hotel, she didn't say anything about it. Maybe she was too tired to say anything about anything. She just gave a faint, flickering smile and closed her eyes, slipping back into sleep.

Ada kept a hand on Mama's shoulder, gazing down at her as she breathed deeply, slowly. Fear rose over her head like a tidal wave, threatening to break over her shoulders and drown her. What if she lost Mama?

She pushed the thought aside. She couldn't lose Mama. She was going to find work, somehow.

She had to.

THERE WAS ONLY one place that Ada could think to go, and it was the park – the same one where she'd watched children playing one day years ago when she'd first decided to become a governess.

As she walked toward the park, she kept her fingers tightly crossed, her heart thumping painfully in her chest. It was a dismal day; the sky was low and grey, threatening rain, and Ada shivered a little, walking as quickly as she could. She couldn't wear her poor threadbare coat – not if she wanted to look presentable in her new dress. The dress had long sleeves, but the fabric, though sturdy, was not designed for the cold of early spring, not without a coat. The wind sliced through it, caressing goosebumps on Ada's skin.

She had been cold ever since taking a wash. It had taken several trips from the pump in the street to the old enamel basin in the tenement to bring enough cold water for Ada to give herself a rudimentary wash. Heating up a fire just to warm some water was an unthinkable waste of fuel. Goose-pimpled and naked, Ada had crouched over the bowl, doing her best with an old rag and the cold water. She felt as though she might never be warm again now.

She smoothed her hands nervously over her hair as she approached the park. There was nothing she could do about the dirt in her hair; putting her head in that cold water would be little less than a death sentence on this day. There was a quiet growl of thunder, but it was not yet raining. Maybe, maybe. Maybe the governesses would still take children to the park today, despite the weather. They needed the fresh air, didn't they?

She took a few nervous little breaths, but the dread mathematics of poverty were circling in her brain. There were only a few pennies left, and no food; she had managed to nurse the soup into Mama, barely. She could buy a few carrots, beets, maybe a potato with the money she had left. It would be enough for two days. Maybe three, if she went without. After that, nothing, and Monday continued to speed toward them like an oncoming train, an imminent collision with disaster.

The park was in front of her. Ada pushed the fearful thoughts from her mind and walked up to the gates, stepping inside, her eyes instantly sweeping over to the duck pond. It was slate grey, reflecting the sky, and the ducks were sculling around contentedly upon it. But they were the only things that moved in the park. There were no happy children playing on the lawns, no governesses sitting on the benches. Nothing.

Ada forced herself to take a few more deep breaths. They would come. It was early. The sky would clear, and they would come, and she would find out from the other governesses how they had gotten their work. Her plan would work. It had to.

She sat down on the bench, folded her hands in her lap, and began to wait. The sky stayed grey. The rain never came, but neither did the sun. And hour after hour ticked by, lonely, silent, the cold slicing through the dress. There was no sound or movement but from the ducks.

Still, Ada sat there, waiting, until darkness fell.

# CHAPTER 16

IT WAS ALMOST a relief that Mama could hardly talk at all that morning. She only wanted to lie on her side, breathing harshly, her body racked from time to time with terrible, raw coughs. She didn't even ask Ada how it had gone the day before; it was as though her last stores of strength, love, and courage had been spent two nights ago when she'd helped Ada with the dress.

Ada had been terrified as she'd spooned tiny mouthfuls of broth into her mother, almost forcing the food into her, but at least it had spared her from telling Mama that she had sat in the park all alone all day, waiting for someone to come, but no one had.

She was still fearful now, her hands clutched in front of her, shaking as she walked toward the front gates of the park. She had sixpence left – that was all. It wouldn't go very far. It might feed them today and tomorrow, but after that, there was nothing. She had to find work... quickly.

She smoothed her hands over the beautiful, rich cloth of her skirt. Today, she promised herself, was the last time she would entertain this governess dream. If there was no hope today, she would go down to the docks and find work selling fish... or herself, if she had to, to save Mama. The thought slid down her back like a piece of ice.

She offered up a trembling prayer. *Please help.* It was all she could manage, but she prayed it silently, over and over, a loop of desperation in her mind.

Walking into the park, Ada saw at once that the duck pond area was empty but for ducks, and that there was nothing even under this sunny sky other than the lawns and the benches. She stumbled to a halt, her heart failing within her chest. For a moment, her head spun, her knees trembling as though they would buckle. It was still early, she knew. She could go and sit on the bench and wait again... and wait... and wait...

The thought was horrifying. Ada couldn't make herself move. She stayed rooted to the spot, her breath coming in tiny, fearful gasps.

Then she heard it: the sound of children laughing.

Overwhelming relief washed over her. Ada turned and saw them: a brood of happy, well-dressed children, with warm coats and hats and neatly polished shoes, were skipping and running down the path toward the park gate. Three or four young governesses followed, most of them a little older than Ada. They were chatting among themselves, carrying parasols, and wearing nice hats, and Ada felt a surge of desperation to be in their company. To be one of them.

But she knew that desperation always appalled the rich. Turning away quickly, she pretended to be examining some early roses, sniffing appreciatively at the buds even though she couldn't care less about their scent. The children and governesses flowed into the park apparently without noticing her, the children scattering to run around the lawns or throw bits of bread to the ducks, causing a chorus of happy quacking.

The children all seemed occupied with their play, and the governesses were all watching their children. One or two of them had sat down to enjoy the sunshine. Ada picked an empty bench and lowered herself slowly onto it, almost holding her breath even as she struggled to act natural. She was within earshot of two of the governesses; one was bouncing a small toddler on her knee, and the other was worriedly watching as two little boys started a wild game of tag around the pond.

"Do be careful, Donald," the worried governess shouted. She had attractive freckles and long, dark hair like Ada's.

"He'll be all right, Milly," said the governess with the toddler.

"I just don't want him to get his socks wet. He had the most dreadful cold last week."

"Oh, the poor thing. He seems much better now, though."

"He is."

The conversation was a quiet, happy little patter, and Ada's heart longed to be one of those women. She gazed at the children, a deep ache starting within her. It would be so wonderful to be with them, listen to their laughter, read to them, pick them up when they cried...

She allowed herself a moment's daydreaming, imagining what it would be like to have children of her very own one day. A baby all her own, that she could cradle in her arms and kiss and cuddle and hold. The ache intensified. She realized that, in her daydream, her baby had Quincy's blue eyes.

*Quincy*. Ada pushed the name out of her mind, even though she longed to sink into it, to open up all those memories, to plunge into the beauty of them. It hurt too much to think of Quincy. She had to try to forget he'd ever existed, even though the thought made everything hurt inside her.

When the girl sat down suddenly beside Ada, she nearly jumped out of her skin. She whipped around to see a pretty girl about her own age with a torrent of yellow hair. The girl wore a lovely blue dress, and she set down a big carpet bag at her feet as she sat beside Ada.

"Whew," she said. "What a morning. It took me half an hour just to get little Ron's shoes onto his feet."

Ada blinked at her, thinking the girl must be speaking to someone else. But when she looked up, laughing as she pushed some hair out of her face, her eyes met Ada's, and she gave her a cheerful smile.

"He was adamant that he was going to the park barefoot. In this weather."

Ada managed a little laugh.

"Happy enough now that he's in the park, of course – shoes and all." The girl gestured toward a tousle-haired little boy who was throwing bread to the ducks. "He loves the ducks. Why, he cried for an hour yesterday when I told him that we couldn't come, poor mite. It looked so much like rain."

"It did," Ada managed, desperate to be part of the conversation. "But it never did rain after all."

"I know. Poor Ron, locked up inside for nothing all day. Well, we'll stay an extra hour in the park today." The girl smiled at her. "You must be new here. I haven't seen you much before."

"I'm Ada."

"Bettina." The girl sat back contentedly, taking in the sunshine. "Have you been a governess very long?"

Ada bit her lip. If she told the truth, she was terrified that Bettina would realize she was nothing but a fraud and leave her. She would have to find out how to become a governess another way.

"No, not very long," she managed, her belly curdling at the lie.

"I've been Ron's governess since he was two. I was just fifteen at the time." Bettina laughed. "Much too young, of course. I doted on that boy and spoiled him a little. Don't spoil your children, Ada – it's a mess."

"Thanks for the advice." Ada smiled, finding herself settling a little in the face of Bettina's relentless friendliness.

"Of course. It's a lonely thing, being a governess. You're not quite a servant but also not quite a member of the family, so you're all alone." Bettina was rummaging in the carpet bag. "I love coming to the park almost as much as Ron does – at least then one can chat with other governesses." She extricated a paper bag and took out a beautiful big white bun, so fresh that Ada could smell it from where she sat. Immediately, Ada's belly cramped with hunger. She hadn't eaten in two days in a bid to keep all their food for Mama.

She forced herself to look away from the bun, even though Bettina was absently tearing it in half, allowing more of its delicious scent to escape.

"So you've been looking after Ron for two or three years, then?" she managed.

"Yes. He's nearly five now. I can hardly believe it." Bettina gave a fond sigh, popping a piece of bread into her mouth and chewing it. "Oh – I hope you don't mind me having a bite while we're sitting here. With the shoe fiasco, I didn't have time for my own breakfast this morning."

"Of course not," said Ada. "Most mornings are just so busy." She managed a little laugh.

"Would you like some? I've got an extra bun in here. Cookie always makes sure I'm well fed, at least," said Bettina. She pulled out another paper bag. "Ron hates bread – he won't touch it. We'll feed it to the ducks otherwise."

Ada stared at the bag, then at Bettina, her heart thudding in her chest. Carefully, somehow, she forced away her desperation. "That's kind of you. Thank you," she said lightly, taking the bag.

"The ducks are quite happy with their stale bread." Bettina chuckled.

"Do you enjoy working for Ron's family, even though it's lonely?" Ada asked, taking a piece of the bread and forcing herself to chew it slowly. "I'm still settling in," she added, to avoid suspicions. "It's my half day off, and I'm here soaking up the sun."

"Oh, yes, I enjoy working for Ron's family. They've been very good to me ever since I was hired."

That was the gap Ada had been looking for. "It's difficult, getting hired," she said, hoping that Bettina would say more.

"Yes, it is. Why, there's hardly any places open at all around here – except for the Caldwells, of course. They've been looking for ages, but that little Bertie is just a terror. He drives governesses away." She laughed.

Ada was listening closely. *Caldwells.* She couldn't imagine that any child would be capable of driving her out of a job that gave her enough money to feed her mother well. "Some children are such a handful," she agreed blandly.

"Not Ron, at least. I was lucky to get him. I got hired very quickly because I had an excellent reference," said Bettina.

Ada's ears pricked. A reference? Her heart faltered a little. She had no one to refer her, no one at all.

"Oh?" she said, keeping her voice casual. "Who referred you?"

"My great-aunt. She's a housekeeper for nobility here in London – very well-known," said Bettina. "I got in with a very good family because of it. I'm very grateful to her. She can be a real old goat, Auntie Cathy, but she looks out for her fellow Edwardses at least. All she had to do was to write a letter to say that she knew me well, and I was hardworking and honest, and I was hired."

Ada let out a slow breath, taking another bite of the bread. Bettina didn't know it, but she had just given Ada the key to her future again.

MAMA WAS WORSE. The sight of her made Ada's heart thump coldly in her throat, like an animated block of ice that she couldn't quite swallow. Mama's eyes were red and sunken, as though her skull was swallowing the last pinpricks of light in them. She lay huddled on her side, the tattered blanket drawn up to her shoulder, staring at nothing. Every breath came with a painful rasp, and Mama would pause occasionally to slide into a fit of appalling coughs that sounded raw and damp.

Ada had faced misgivings about her plan all through the walk back home. The dishonesty didn't sit well with her. But the sight of Mama was enough to banish all of her misgivings: nothing she could do would be worse than allowing her mother to...

She didn't allow herself to think the word *die*. Mama looked so sick that it felt as though mentioning Death's name would bring the Reaper hurrying all the more quickly to her bedside. Instead, she forced herself to smile as she let the curtain of the tenement fall closed behind her and crouched down beside her mother.

"Mama, I'm home," she whispered. "And I'm going to make you some lovely tea."

Mama's tortured eyes turned up to Ada's. She reached up with a trembling hand to touch Ada's cheek. "The fever... it's hard..." She blinked. "When did you get so grown up and so beautiful?"

Ada's heart squeezed at those words. She knew Mama was delirious with fever, but she could treasure the little moment and the small compliment, nonetheless.

"I spoke with a governess today, Mama. She was ever so friendly, and she told me what I have to do to get a job. I'm sure I'll have a position before very long."

But Mama wasn't listening anymore. She rolled onto her side again and resumed her trembling, silent huddle, locked in the world of her own suffering.

Ada gritted her teeth. She set the pot over the meagre fire to boil some water, then sat down in front of one of the wooden boxes and carefully extracted a small sheet of paper and a pen from her coat pocket. She knew that the paper was cheap and rough, but at least it was mostly clean; the pen had cost a small fortune, even though it was just a cracked old thing with only a few drops of ink left in it, but Ada knew that using a pencil would be useless.

She gave another glance at her mother and thought regretfully of sweet, sweet Bettina. Surely this wouldn't get her in any kind of trouble, however. The only person standing to lose something from this deception was Ada – and she would risk it to save Mama.

She took a deep breath and began to write.

*Dear Sir and Madam,*

*It pleases me to refer to you the bearer of this letter, Miss Ada Carter, a young woman of excellent character whom I know through my great-niece, Bettina...*

Ada's toes curled as she continued writing in her best, most flowing script, writing in a way she hadn't written since leaving the Morgan house. She prayed as she wrote, trying to be honest about her own strengths, her heart thudding against her chest. This was their only real hope.

*She will prove to be an excellent governess to you, and I wish her all the best.*

*Yours sincerely,*

*Mrs. Catherine Edwards.*

Ada signed the letter with what she imagined would be Mrs. Edwards' signature – a flowing and florid thing – and then blew on it softly to dry the ink. She knew that she'd committed a dreadful wrong.

But she also knew she had no other choice... and that even this might not work.

# CHAPTER 17

NUMBER 73, Hollyhock Avenue, was so tall and extravagant and imposing that Ada almost turned around and went straight home at once. In fact, if she hadn't grown up in a similar home with the Morgans, she might have been far too daunted even to take another step.

As it was, she hesitated on the sidewalk, staring up at the little path leading around to the servants' entrance. It wasn't the size or splendour of the house, necessarily, that was giving her pause. The Morgan house had been about the same: it, too, had three towering stories, and a lush green garden, and pine trees surrounding it like tall, dark sentinels. She could guess the layout of this house by looking at it: the kitchens and scullery, the servants' quarters, the dining room, drawing room, parlour, studies, library, bedrooms, perhaps even a small ballroom like the Morgans had had. Ada even knew that it was considered humble of a governess to use the servants' entrance, even though she would walk through the main doors when she accompanied the master's children. She smoothed a hand down over her green dress, determined to make a good impression.

No, it wasn't the size of the house that was making her hesitate. It was the memories. Looking up at this house brought back her daydreams of a time when she'd lived in a home such as this one. Oh, there were things she missed about the house itself, of course − the warm baths, the clean clothes, always being in front of a nice, crackling fire on a wet winter's day. Never going hungry. Drinking chocolate and eating roast goose. But most of all, she realized, her heart stinging within her, she missed Mama's smile and Quincy's laugh.

She closed her eyes for a second to hold back her tears and took a steadying breath. Quincy was long gone, but maybe this house would be part of bringing back Mama's smile.

Squaring her shoulders, Ada marched forward, up the pathway and to the servants' door. She knocked twice, then waited politely. Distantly, she could hear raised voices in one of the other rooms. One of them was high-pitched − a child's. Chillingly, she remembered what Bettina had said about the Caldwells' little boy.

She knocked again. This time, the door swung open to reveal a very frazzled, red-faced kitchen maid.

"Who are you?" the maid demanded.

Ada swallowed. "My name is..."

"I don't care what your name is," barked the maid. "What do you want?"

Ada took a steadying breath. "I would like to apply for the position of governess."

"Oh, thank goodness," cried the maid. She grabbed Ada's arm. "This way."

Surprised by the overenthusiastic reception, Ada nonetheless allowed herself to be more or less dragged through the kitchen. The yelling intensified; Ada recognized it as the sound of a small child having a shocking temper tantrum.

"He's been screamin' for an hour," said the maid. "No one can hush him and the master's about to lose his mind. We're all about to lose our minds. The last governess left two weeks ago, and it's been all but impossible."

She pulled open a large door and shoved Ada into a hallway. "Good luck," she said and disappeared.

Ada was left in the hall on her own, listening to the child's deafening shrieks.

"I don't WANT a nap. I don't. I don't. I don't."

This was all very strange, Ada thought. She'd been conducted here by a kitchen-maid – where was the butler, the house-keeper, even the parlourmaid? She wondered if she would get into trouble for being here, if her chances were gone before they'd even started. Her hands trembled on the faked letter of recommendation that she clutched in both hands.

"You will go to bed at once." thundered an irate feminine voice, thick with good breeding. "This is your last chance, Albert. Get up off the floor and go to your room, or I'll take the birch switch to you."

"No, no, please, don't," cried a delicate voice.

The child let out a long, wordless shriek that was tainted with frustration, confusion, and tiredness. The sound clutched at Ada's heart. Before she could stop herself, she was walking down the hallway toward it and turning through the open doors of a large dining room. The debris of a finished meal still lay on the table − cups and plates, crumbs and cutlery − and beside the long wooden table a small boy lay on his front, feet kicking, fists pummelling the rich carpet.

He was surrounded by a crew of adults, all of them looking equally bewildered. The woman in an elegant black dress was red-faced and furious, her neatly braided hair in disarray; the housekeeper, Ada guessed. She was waving a finger at the child and shouting. The mistress was hovering to one side, her tasteful eye makeup streaming down her powdered cheeks as she sobbed and wrung her thin, white hands. The butler in his tailcoat was somewhere nearby, looking as though the mistress had ordered him to be there, but he was none too happy about it.

"I'm telling you right now, Albert, you are to get to your feet this instant or there will be consequences," thundered the housekeeper, raising her hand in a threatening manner.

"No, no," sobbed the mistress. "No, please, don't touch him."

"Get up, young sir," barked the butler. "Don't you know you're in for a beating if you don't?"

The child continued shrieking. "I shan't take a nap. I shan't. I shan't. Not without my story."

"Mama will read you a story, my dearest little treasure, my sweet little poppet," mewed the mistress.

"No. I want Nurse to read me the story about the rabbit," howled the child, red-faced, strings of saliva dribbling from his shouting mouth. "I want the rabbit story. Rabbit story."

"Can't you just read him the story?" the butler muttered to the housekeeper.

"He wants Nurse – even though she's been gone two years now. And besides, I don't know what story he's talking about," barked the housekeeper. "I've never seen such a book in the nursery."

"RABBIT STORY," howled the child.

The housekeeper raised her hand, but before she could land a blow, Ada was scurrying across the floor. She crouched down beside the little boy and held up her hands as though reading a book.

"Once upon a time," she pretended to read, "there was a little rabbit."

The child paused in his shrieks to look up at her for a moment.

"Who are you?" demanded the housekeeper.

"How did you get in?" barked the butler.

The child began to scream again.

"For pity's sake," cried the mistress. "Leave her be – she's quietening him."

Ada felt a surge of hope. Her hands shaking, praying that this would work, she cleared her throat and went on.

"The little rabbit lived in an enchanted wood," she read, "and he loved to play in the fairy glens with the primroses and the pixies, the sunflowers and the sprites."

The child's cries slowed to a whimper. He rolled onto his side and looked up at Ada, his eyes very round. Somehow, it was working.

"Keep going," whispered the mistress.

"This is ridiculous mollycoddling," mumbled the housekeeper.

Still, she didn't seem about to stop Ada, so Ada went on, turning the invisible page of her invisible book. This wrung a little giggle from the child.

"One day, the little rabbit was tired from dancing and frisking about in the glens with all of his fairy friends," she said. "His eyes felt scratchy, and his feet were sore. His legs ached, and even his fluffy little tail was starting to cramp."

The child was listening with wide, teary-eyed, reddened from the tantrum.

"What do you think the little rabbit did next?" Ada asked the child.

He rubbed an eye with his knuckles and shook his head.

"Well, the little rabbit's head and feet and eyes hurt, so he started to stamp about. 'Ouch,' he said. 'My feet hurt. My eyes are sore.'" She turned another invisible page. "Then a friend of his, a very wise fairy, came fluttering down beside him."

"Was she a pretty fairy?" asked the child.

"A very pretty fairy, with a yellow dress made from butter-cups," said Ada. "She said, 'Don't worry, little rabbit. I can help you feel better.'"

"Did she help him?"

"Of course, she did. She took the rabbit by the hand and led him to a little hollow filled with autumn leaves. She lined the hollow with feathers from their bird friends, and a bit of fluffy hair from their mouse friends, and she made a pillow from spider-silk. Then the little rabbit lay down in his nice, soft bed, and the wise fairy put a big green leaf over him." Ada smiled. "And the little rabbit had a nice, long nap."

The child pouted a little. "I hate naps."

"No one likes naps," said Ada seriously. "But do you know what happened when the little rabbit woke?"

"What?"

"He felt a thousand times better." Ada turned the imaginary page. "He started to jump and frisk and play all over again, with strong feet and bright eyes, and even the cramp was gone from his fluffy little tail." She pretended to turn the book around. "See? There's a picture of him."

The child giggled. "There's no picture," he said.

"Oh?" Ada pretended to look down at the book in amazement. "Well. I suppose I'll have to teach you how to see invisible things."

Her breath caught at those words, and she shot a worried glance up at the mistress. She'd been so caught up in soothing the child that she'd forgotten these people – who could change her life – were standing right there beside her. Her words were presumptuous, she knew...

"Mama, I think I'll go up for my nap now with Mrs. Jonas," said the child imperiously.

There was an air of palpable relief in the room. Mrs. Jonas didn't even complain about the little boy's manners. She just took his hand and led him away, and Ada felt suddenly naked and alone now that she didn't have the child with her. The butler was staring at her with cold eyes, and she straightened up quickly, folding her hands in front of her.

"I apologize for coming into your dining room unannounced, sir," she said, her heart pounding as she gave her best little curtsy. "Your maid showed me in."

"And why should she do that?" demanded the butler.

"I – I told her that I was here about the open position." She cleared her throat. "For a governess. I have my reference here."

She held out her letter, and the mistress took it, opening it hastily and skimming over it. "Oh – Mrs. Edwards. I've heard of her," she whispered in a reverential tone. Then she looked up at Ada. "What's your name, child?"

"Ada Carter, if you please, ma'am."

"Well, Miss Carter, you're hired. Can you start at once?"

Ada stared at her for a few long seconds, her mouth opening and shutting. She had been striving for this for two long years, yet part of her had never believed that it could happen. And it had happened. And she could hardly breathe.

The mistress clutched at one of her hands. "Forgive me, Miss Carter, I know this is all very unorthodox – but – well – my Bertie is... not an easy child." Her cheeks flushed a little. "His papa travels all the time for business, and we hardly ever see him, and..." She trailed off. "You shall have twenty-seven pounds a year, and your room and board besides."

Ada's heart leaped in her chest. She wanted to cry out in joy, perhaps to throw her arms around the mistress's neck and kiss her, but all of that would be grossly inappropriate. Somehow containing her trembling excitement, she managed a smile.

"Thank you, ma'am," she said as calmly as she could. "That would be very sufficient."

# PART IV

# CHAPTER 18

*ONE YEAR Later*

"THAT'S IT, BERTIE," said Ada, smiling down at her young charge. "Now try another one."

Bertie looked up at her with his big, brown eyes. They could be so tempestuous at times, yet now they held a calm, liquid depth that always stirred Ada's heart. He gave her a little smile, his plump red cheeks dimpling appealingly, and looked back down at his slate. With his chubby fist clenched around his slate pencil, he painstakingly scratched out a fat letter D.

"D for dog," he said proudly, pointing at the ancient poodle that lay sleeping in its basket by the hearth.

"Bertie, that's wonderful." Ada clapped her hands, laughing with pleasure. This was a new connection that he'd made on his own; she'd used the word *duck* to teach him the D sound. "Yes, D is for dog."

Bertie grinned, then paused, rubbing his eyes. Ada glanced at the big grandfather clock in the corner of the nursery. "I think it's time for your nap, my love," she said, getting up from her chair.

Bertie yawned. "All right," he said demurely.

Ada gathered him into her arms and carried him over to his bed, her heart bursting with pride. The other governesses who gathered in the park from time to time had told her that they barely recognized Bertie compared to the way he had been before she'd become his governess. She cuddled the child against her, sitting him down on his little bed and then bending down to untie his shoes. He had become her pride and joy.

He fell asleep almost instantly once she had him nicely settled in bed, which was her cue to go downstairs for her own lunch. The parlourmaid was in the room right next door, and she would ring for Ada if Bertie woke early. But Bertie almost never woke early; Ada had thirty precious minutes to spare, and she knew exactly where she wanted to spend them.

She hurried down the stairs as gracefully as she could, keeping a hand on the banister, chin up, back straight. It was surprising how quickly all of these things had come back to her now that she was living in a grand house again. In a few moments, she was trotting down the steps into the kitchen.

It was quiet in here; the kitchen staff themselves were snatching a few precious minutes of rest after lunch and before supper, and everything was tidied away, set right, ready for the evening chaos. The only thing out of place was a small plate on the kitchen table, covered with a little napkin. From the direction of the pantry, Ada could hear the soft hiss of a broom on the floor.

She paused, ignoring the plate despite the grumble of hunger in her belly. "Mama?"

The sweeping stopped, and Mama emerged from the pantry in her tired maid's uniform, the knees of the white apron worn so thin that Ada could see the black skirt underneath. As always, she felt a painful sting through her heart and a rush of relief at the same time. It broke her to see Mama bundled into a maid's uniform like this, especially when Ada herself was neatly dressed, as a governess ought to be. But at least Mama's cheeks were pink, and her eyes were bright, and she even managed a small smile when she saw Ada standing by the table.

"There's your lunch, dear," she said.

"Thank you, Mama." Ada sat down and pulled the plate nearer, ravenous. "Have you had lunch yet?"

"Yes, thank you, darling."

"And are you sure you had enough?" Ada asked, as she always did.

Mama smiled. "Yes, thank you," she said.

Ada hoped it was true. She was so glad that, after weeks of pleading, she had managed to get Mama into this position as a scullery-maid. At the same time, her heart ached that a woman like her would be stuck doing this work, normally reserved for ten- or twelve-year-old girls with their entire future ahead of them.

"Someday, Mama, I'll find my way up in the world," she said. "I'll take you to a cottage of our own, and you'll never have to work another stitch in all your life."

Mama just gave her a fluttering smile. "Marry well, my dear," she said. "That's all you can really do."

Ada dropped her eyes to hide her blush. She was sixteen now, and the other governesses were all talking about the young men they were seeing, the men they hoped to marry, their hope and dreams for domestic life one day.

She couldn't say she didn't share in those dreams. But in her heart of hearts, she knew she would only ever be an old maid.

The only alternative was an utter impossibility.

IMPOSSIBILITY OR NOT, that Sunday afternoon, Ada's feet still carried her down the broad and clean-swept streets of upper-class London toward the home that had once been her own.

Sunday afternoons were the only time Ada really had to herself. Mrs. Caldwell always wanted to spend time with Bertie herself after church, and she would take him to the park or the theatre. Bertie didn't like the theatre at all, but Ada had talked him into going; she knew that Mrs. Caldwell relished every minute she spent with her little boy, even if she hopelessly spoiled him.

That left Ada free to do as she pleased, and there was only one thing she really wanted to do apart from caring for Bertie and her mother, even though she knew that it was nothing but a fool's errand.

She kept her parasol neatly cocked on her shoulder, occasionally tucking a few stray hairs back underneath her hat. Part of her hoped she might be unrecognizable now that she'd grown into a young lady, now that she was nicely dressed and properly fed. After all, even if he did recognize her, what would she say to him? What could he do? She was still just a governess. And if he knew how she'd become a governess at all... Her stomach clenched, and she thrust the thought out of her mind.

No, it was better for her never to speak to Quincy Morgan again. She'd accepted that. Yet somehow every Sunday afternoon her feet still carried her to the neighbourhood of

Morgan House, and she found herself always watchful for him, hoping just to see him one last time. Just to hear his laugh and know that he had somehow overcome the loss of his mother and his best friend in the same week all those years ago.

She was strolling along the edge of the park near their home now. It was far larger than the park where she took Bertie to feed the ducks and occasionally waved at Bettina; this one had a bridle path going round it and was always filled with upper-class people riding their hacks. Quincy had always wanted to ride in the park when he was a little boy, but Sophia was afraid of horses and never let him, and, of course, Master Simon was never around to go with him.

Ada's feet were aching after a long week of running around after her busy little charge. She sighed regretfully, looking down the road toward the Morgan house. It was another half-hour's walk down there, and for what? To pass by the front gate, and look up longingly toward the house that held so many memories? She'd done it a few times, hoping to see Quincy, but, of course, he was never outside. Why would he be?

A leaden weariness swept over her, and Ada turned and plodded into the park itself. In her neat-enough dress, she wouldn't be thrown outside, at any rate. She sat herself down on a low wall running by the bridle path and swung her sore feet, enjoying the soft sunshine that poured down over her. There were a few ladies and gentlemen riding past on their elegant horses; some children too, on fat, fluffy ponies. Bertie wanted a pony. Ada smiled at the thought of him trotting along on a lead rein behind a stablemaster. Maybe she could persuade Mrs. Caldwell to get him a pony, if only in honour of Quincy.

There was a sudden flutter of wings. Ada jumped, turning, as some pigeons burst out of one of the nearby bushes and swooped off into the blue April sky. Hooves clattered; a startled chestnut horse rose suddenly on his hind legs, shoes flashing as he pawed at the air.

"Whoa, Conqueror," cried a strangely familiar voice. The young gentleman astride the horse leaned forward, trying to balance. "Whoa, boy."

But the chestnut was thoroughly frightened. He landed from his rear and leaped into the air, spinning around. Most gentlemen would have kept their seat effortlessly, but this one was already half falling, a stirrup swinging free of his foot.

"Oh," cried Ada, jumping to her feet at the sight of the imminent disaster.

"Whoa," cried the gentleman, despairingly, but the horse launched up onto his hind legs again and the gentleman was tipped clean out of the saddle. He met the ground on his back with a resounding crash, and the horse galloped off, stirrups and reins flapping.

"Oh," Ada gasped again.

"I'll catch him," cried the gentleman's companion, setting spurs to his own horse and galloping off in pursuit of the chestnut.

That left the poor young gentleman lying on the ground, his face very white, groaning in pain. Ada tossed aside her parasol and ran over to him. "Sir? Sir," she cried, crouching down beside him. "Are you all right? Are you hurt?"

The gentleman squinted up at her against the sunlight. "Yes," he ground out. "Ugh. Just – winded." He writhed on the ground.

"Let me help you up." Ada grasped his arm, pulling him into a sitting position. "There now. You'll catch your breath in a minute and feel better."

The young gentleman covered his face with one hand and took a long, shaky breath.

"Are you hurt, sir?" Ada asked.

He seemed to have caught his breath for the most part. "No," he said at length, taking another deep, shaky breath. "Thank you. I'm quite all right." He cleared his throat, lowering his hand. "Well – apart from having made the most ridiculous fool of myself in front of a lovely lady."

Ada laughed. "Don't worry about that, sir. I'm glad you're not hurt. Let me help you up."

She took a firm grip of his arm, and the young gentleman wobbled to his feet. "My father never took me out to ride with him as a child, you see," he said, reaching up to straighten his hat. "Seems as though I'm still catching up. In any case – thank you."

He turned to face her, and suddenly Ada's breath hitched in her chest, and she was painfully aware that she was still holding his arm in one hand, that his eyes were the bluest blue she'd ever seen, paler than the sea, deeper than the sky, that it was him, finally him, and she was looking up into the face of her only true friend.

"Quincy?" she breathed.

His eyes widened, and something flared in them. He stepped closer to her, reached forward as though to embrace her, then rested his hands on her shoulders instead. "Ada," he gasped. "Could it be you?"

"Yes. It's me." Tears filled Ada's cheeks, and she blinked at them furiously. "It's me."

"You look so well." Quincy burst out. He made no effort to stop his own tears, which burst down his cheeks. "Oh, Ada, for so many years I've thought – after seeing you in rags – going back to search for you..." His tears came faster. "I thought you were dead... but here you are. Alive. Well. Beautiful." He stumbled over the last word, as though it came out by accident.

"I'm a governess for the Caldwells," said Ada, laughing up at him. "Oh, Quincy, I can't believe it's you."

"Master Morgan."

Quincy's body stiffened. He dropped his hands from her shoulders at once, wiping furiously at his tears.

"I have to go," he said. "Papa is expecting me."

The way he said it made a cold chill run through Ada's spine. She stumbled forward, plucking at his sleeve. "Quincy – wait. Are you all right?"

He gave her a haunted look, a vulnerable and wounded thing, and it made her stomach clench in fear for him. But he covered it quickly with a cocky, suave smile, the kind of expression she'd never seen on his face before.

"I'm taking over Papa's company," he said with a hollow pride in his tone. "I'm doing very well, thank you. Don't worry about me."

It had been years since she'd spoken to him, but she could still tell at once when he was lying. "Quincy…"

"I must be going. I see Wilson has caught my horse." Quincy ran his hands over his jacket, smoothing it briskly.

Ada's heart ached for him. For all the fuss he was putting on now, she could see the frightened little boy behind his eyes.

"I work for the Caldwells," she said abruptly. "If you ever... if you..." She didn't know how to finish.

Quincy was already walking away, and it felt as though he was tearing out a piece of her heart as he moved. But, suddenly he stopped, turned to face her, and she saw the old Quincy in his eyes again for a moment: the softness in him, the sparkle.

"It was wonderful to see you, Ada," he said softly. "Truly."

She believed he meant every word. But it still didn't stop him from walking away, his back very straight, looking dead ahead, as though he was making every effort not to turn around and look back.

THE OTHER SERVANTS all thought that Sally, the housemaid, was nothing but a hopeless chatterbox, yet Ada quite liked her. It alleviated some of the quiet loneliness that draped many of Ada's hours; she loved Bertie, yet often found herself hungering for adult company. Apart from a precious few moments with her mother, she hardly ever spoke to another grown person.

It was a rare treat for her, then, when Sally happened to be cleaning the nursery at the same time as Ada and Bertie were inside it. Normally Sally would do her duties while Ada was taking Bertie out for his daily walk, but it was miserable and raining outside today, and so Bertie was playing contentedly with some blocks on the hearth rug while Ada mended a split seam in one of his little trousers. Ada was now proficient in working a needle, which often came in handy.

Sally bustled around the room, dusting, changing the linen, packing away Bertie's clean clothes. And she was never silent even for a moment, a constant stream of gossip, speculation and empty chatter pouring from her. It was as good as going to the theatre, Ada would guess, not that she had ever been there.

"And did you hear that Poppy's been in trouble again for being seen with that young man from the house next door?" Sally prattled on. "Why, Mrs. Caldwell has already given her a warning about that – she's furious now. I don't think Poppy can make too many more mistakes before she finds herself in serious trouble."

"Is that so?" said Ada, feigning indifference, although her mind launched at once into a series of calculations. Poppy was Mrs. Caldwell's lady's maid, and if she left, the parlourmaid would likely step into her position. That would mean that Mama might have a chance at becoming the parlourmaid. Ada thought of Mama's wrinkles and stooped figure and sighed. Parlourmaids were normally chosen to be pretty young girls.

"It is and all. Foolish Poppy – although I suppose one can hardly blame her, being twenty-two years old already. Why, how are we ever meant to marry if we're never allowed to see any young men?" She laughed. "I don't suppose you have a secret beau hiding somewhere, Ada?"

Ada thought of Quincy, and her heart stung. She managed a faint smile. "I'm afraid not, Sally."

"Oh, well. At any rate, there'll be a man about the house again soon enough."

A cold jolt ran through Ada. She lifted her head. "A man?"

"That's right. Mrs. Caldwell has hired a valet. That can only mean one thing – Mr. Caldwell must be coming back from America."

Ada swallowed hard, her mouth suddenly very dry. She wondered if Mr. Caldwell knew that his wife had hired a new governess in his absence, if he would check up on her references, perhaps write to Mrs. Edwards and find out that she had no knowledge that any Ada Carter even existed...

She took a quiet breath to calm herself as Sally's chatter continued. Why would he? Mr. Caldwell would be content with his wife's hiring, she was sure. Especially since Bertie was so much happier these days. She stared down at the little boy where he played on the rug, her fluttering heart soothing. Surely... surely Mr. Caldwell had other things to worry about and wouldn't start questioning his governess out of the blue.

"When do you think he'll be back?" Ada asked as casually as she could.

"I can't think it'll be long. Mrs. Jonas is interviewing valets today; she seems in a bit of a hurry. Well, I'm sure Mrs. Caldwell will be glad – Mr. Caldwell was supposed to have been gone only until the winter, after all."

Ada knew that full well. It had felt like a stay of execution when Mrs. Caldwell had told her that her husband had been forced to winter in America; but the stay was over now, and Ada could feel the tenuous happiness she'd built over the past few months wobbling dangerously as she thought of Mr. Caldwell's return.

She took a long breath to soothe her jangling nerves and focused on her work. What more could she do? It was out of her hands now. Still, a little voice of worry continued to nibble and nibble at the edges of her consciousness.

# CHAPTER 19

BERTIE LOOKED HIS VERY BEST. Scrubbed and prepared as though for church on a Sunday morning, the little boy's face glowed pink from washing, and Ada had dressed him in his best little suit and tie. She thought that there was nothing in the world more adorable than Bertie in his best clothes, with his dapper little coat and his shiny little shoes. She smoothed a hand over his hair, making sure that it was neatly combed and slicked down.

"This tie is so tight," Bertie complained. "Can't I take it off? It's hot."

"Not yet, darling," said Ada. "You have to look your very best for your papa, now."

Bertie had regarded his father's return with apathy, not unlike the way Quincy had felt about Master Simon coming home from India back when they were both children.

"I don't want to look my best for Papa. He never gives me sweets or plays with me," said Bertie.

"Your papa's very busy, that's all. He still loves you," said Ada, not sure that it was true. It certainly hadn't been for Quincy.

Bertie looked about to complain some more, but Ada had been working on his ability to be cheerful, so he took a deep breath and visibly decided to buck up. She took his hand and led him down the staircase, where the servants were all lining up in a parade of sorts to welcome the master down.

Ada and the little one, of course, had pride of place right behind Mrs. Caldwell. The graceful woman was standing at the bottom of the steps, with the drive leading up to the front door. She had an air of desperation wrapped around her, as tight as the extravagant red gown she wore, its plunging neckline and embroidered bodice screaming for attention.

"Be very good now, Bertie, dear," Mrs. Caldwell quavered.

"Yes, Mama," said Bertie.

Ada squeezed his hand and smiled down at him, feeling a tickle of nervousness as she shook out the skirts of her own tidy but modest dress. She took a few deep breaths, trying to look the picture of a calm, composed governess.

There was a great clattering of hooves. Everyone stiffened, from the butler in his coattails to Mama in her maid's uniform. Mama had her bonnet pulled down low in an effort to keep Mr. Caldwell from seeing how old she was. Ada shot her a sympathetic glance, and then the master's carriage came charging up the driveway. It was pulled by a four-in-hand of flashy black horses, perfectly matched, their knees flying high as they charged toward the house with thundering feet.

The carriage rattled to a halt, the footman jumped down smartly to open the door, and Mr. Caldwell stepped out, blinking in the spring sunlight, and swinging a smart walking stick. He was an aggressively handsome man; the streak of grey in his neatly cut hair only served to command submission, an effect heightened by the smoothly chiselled lines of his jaw, cheek and brow, the piercing quality of his grey eyes, and the smartly clipped moustache that stood to attention on his upper lip.

His grey eyes swept the gathering, lingering for a moment on Ada, traveling up and down her body in a way that made her tremble to the pit of her stomach. She swallowed hard.

"My darling, I'm so glad to see you." cried Mrs. Caldwell, flinging herself at her husband and throwing her arms around him.

"Now, now, my dear," murmured Mr. Caldwell, staring at Ada for a moment longer before directing his gaze back toward his wife.

"Was your journey safe?" asked Mrs. Caldwell.

"Good enough, thank you, although we hit a patch of rough seas soon after leaving New York."

"You must be exhausted, darling. Let's retire to the parlour for some coffee before lunch, shall we?" Mrs. Caldwell forced an arm through her husband's. "Oh – and look how darling Bertie has grown, my love."

Mr. Caldwell went over to his son and gave him a courteous smile. "Good morning, young sir," he said formally, reaching out a hand.

Bertie withdrew, hiding behind Ada's skirts.

"Bertie, darling, it's Papa," said Ada gently. "Greet him politely." She trembled inwardly, terrified that Mr. Caldwell would take Bertie's shyness as her personal failure to instil manners in the boy.

To her utter relief, Bertie emerged from behind her skirts and stared up at his father with round eyes. "Hello, Papa."

"That's a good boy," said Mr. Caldwell, with sudden warmth. He reached down and squeezed Bertie's little hand. Overwhelmed, the little boy ducked behind Ada's skirts again.

"Bertie," Ada hissed.

"And who is this... *nice* young lady?" Mr. Caldwell asked, straightening up to look Ada in the eye. He was not very tall, but his presence radiated something – power, perhaps. Ada wasn't sure she liked it, but she was overwhelmingly relieved to hear a good word spoken about her. Maybe he wouldn't investigate her after all. Her anxious heart stilled somewhat.

Mrs. Caldwell's lips were pursed, her eyes shooting Ada a furious glance as she responded. "This is Miss Carter, dear, our new governess."

"Ah, a new governess." Mr. Caldwell held out a hand. "Delighted to meet you, lovely Miss Carter."

Ada hesitated a second before she shook his hand, and it was a strong, possessing grip that took ownership of her entire hand.

"Pleased to meet you, sir," she said.

He smiled, showing all of his teeth. "The pleasure's all mine, I assure you," he said.

Mrs. Caldwell plucked at his arm. "Come on now, darling."

Mr. Caldwell allowed himself to be led away into the house, and Ada let out a long breath. He was happy with her. He wouldn't pry into the circumstances that led to her appointment as his son's governess.

She should be relieved, and yet as she watched him go, Ada felt a knot of fear growing like a tumour in her stomach.

ADA CRACKED the nursery door open just a little, peering cautiously down the long hallway with its dark shadows cast by the patterned wallpaper and portraits on the walls. Bertie was fast asleep; the nursery was dark and quiet except for the golden crackle of the fireplace. Her duties were done for tonight, and she was ready to retire to her own room, which was at the end of the hallway – on the other side of the bedrooms and upstairs drawing-room. It was close enough that she would hear Bertie if he called for her, but definitely far enough to make it very clear that she was no member of this family.

Still, that room seemed to be a thousand miles away tonight. Things had been so odd ever since Mr. Caldwell had returned. Wherever her master and mistress went, Bertie suddenly had to go too, whether it was a stroll around the park or a trip to the marketplace to be measured for new clothing. The child was tired of it, and Ada was struggling to keep him cheerful – especially with Mr. Caldwell's distracting eyes on her for every moment, and Mrs. Caldwell's increasing sharpness with her.

And tonight, Mrs. Caldwell wasn't home at all. She'd gone off to the opera with her friends, and Mr. Caldwell had decided at the last moment that he wasn't going with her. Ada could see the pool of gold light falling from the drawing-room into the hallway. He was in there, she knew; smoking and reading, and she couldn't shake off the feeling that he was waiting for her somehow. The echoes of the empty house around her made her belly hurt with nervousness. All the other servants would be downstairs now, finishing up in the stables and kitchen. Ada was alone.

Well, she couldn't stay here in the nursery all night. She took a deep breath, squaring her shoulders and pushing aside her silly fears. Mr. Caldwell had always been good to her – and, to her eternal gratitude, he hadn't tried to find out more about her past even though he'd been home for three weeks now. She was safe.

She stepped out of the nursery, closing the door as quietly as possible even though Bertie could sleep through practically anything. Her feet silent on the carpet, Ada headed toward her room, her hands clenched nervously in front of her. It wasn't that far away. In a moment, she'd be safely tucked up in bed. It was all going to be just fine.

She passed the drawing-room door, not daring to look inside. Warm firelight splashed over her, and then she was past it and heading to her room, and everything was –

"Miss Carter?"

Ada kept walking, her heart thudding painfully in the back of her throat. She would pretend she hadn't heard him.

"Miss Carter." called Mr. Caldwell.

Ada stopped. She was shaking now, and for a moment she considered rushing to her room and locking herself inside. But no. That would cost her the job – the job that kept Mama safe and warm and well-fed. Ada took another sip of air, squared her shoulders, and marched up to the drawing-room door.

"Good evening, Mr. Caldwell," she said politely. "Do you need anything?"

Mr. Caldwell was lounging in a deep armchair, smoking a cigar. Wisps of blue smoke curled from his mouth and nose, the smell acrid and expensive. Ada didn't like it. He didn't look up at her, just drew deeply on his cigar again before responding.

"Why don't you come in, dear?" he asked. "Warm yourself by the fire."

"Thank you, sir, but there's a fire in my room. It's quite warm, I assure you."

He gestured languidly. "Sit anyway," he said, and there was an edge to his tone that raised goosebumps on Ada's arm.

She shuffled forward, choosing a chair on the furthest side of the room from Mr. Caldwell. He turned his head, his attention suddenly and disconcertingly locked upon her as she sank into her seat. Again, his eyes moved over her, roving without restraint. She reached up and tucked her shawl a little closer around her neck.

He let out a deep chuckle, sucked on the cigar again. "How old are you, Miss Carter? ... Ada? May I call you Ada?"

Ada swallowed, suddenly uncomfortable with the sound of her own name. "As you wish, sir."

He smirked. "Well, how old are you, Ada?"

Ada was used to lying about her age; she'd done it on her phony reference, after all. "Eighteen, sir."

"I could swear you looked younger."

Ada swallowed hard, holding down her nervousness, and managed a smile. "I've always looked younger than my age, sir."

"I suppose." Mr. Caldwell chuckled, leaning forward, and huffed out another cloud of the rich, expensive smoke. "Still... I do like a younger girl."

Ada drew back a little, tucking herself into her chair. "Mrs. Caldwell suits you very nicely, sir."

Mr. Caldwell gave a harsh laugh. "Oh, Mrs. Caldwell." He took a deep breath of smoke, then snorted it dismissively. "She's nothing compared to a... pretty young thing." He was on the edge of his seat now, reaching over the gap between them, and laid a hand on her knee. The fingers tightened around her leg, and his eyes bored into hers. "Like you," he whispered huskily, the smoke blowing into her eyes.

Ada recoiled. "I don't take your meaning, sir," she quavered to buy herself some time, although she took his meaning perfectly well.

"Oh, I think you do, young lady." Mr. Caldwell leaned all the way forward, the smoke making a veil between them, his hand traveling up her leg. "No one is home. No one need ever know."

For a trembling instant, Ada thought of Mama, and she stayed frozen where she was even with Mr. Caldwell's wandering hand, even though he had risen from his chair and was standing over her, the cigar smoke draping her in dizzy confusion. She knew that if she only stayed still, her position – and Mama's – would be safe...

Then his hand wandered too far, and Ada couldn't take it. She lunged out of the chair, diving out of the cloud of smoke, and sucking down the fresh air.

"Sir," she cried.

Mr. Caldwell's eyes glimmered dangerously as he took the cigar from his lips and stared at her. "Think carefully before you do this," he growled.

"Please, sir." Ada swallowed hard. "Please, I'm only a governess." She knew, suddenly and painfully, why all those other governesses had left. Bertie had never been the problem.

Mr. Caldwell studied her with glittering eyes. "Come back here, Ada."

She knew that if she did, there would be no escape. She backed toward the door. "I'm sorry, sir, but I must go."

"You'll be sorry," Mr. Caldwell hissed.

She knew she would, saw it in his eyes that she would, but everything in her was screaming at her to just get out of the room and away from this man. Hitching up her skirts, she turned and fled to her room, running down the hall, slamming the door, and locking it tightly. Then she sat on her bed, breathing hard, the key clenched in both her trembling fists.

# CHAPTER 20

"It's such a nice day today," babbled Mrs. Caldwell. "I think we'll take Bertie out to the park for a bit. Don't you think that would be nice, dear?"

Mr. Caldwell answered only with a grunt of indifference. The chilling temperature in the room seemed to drop a few more degrees; Ada felt that she was being suffocated in a cold fist of pressure. She brushed a tiny speck of lint from Bertie's shoulder, wondering why the boy had been summoned to his parents' breakfast table when he almost always ate in the nursery.

She was standing attentively behind Bertie's chair, her own breakfast of porridge lying heavily in her stomach while the Caldwells enjoyed ham and toast, eggs, and fruit. Bertie pushed his scrambled eggs around his place without much interest, then set down his fork. "May I be excused to go and play, Miss Ada?" he asked.

Normally, Ada would rejoice at his excellent little display of manners, and she was just as eager to get out of the cold silence of the dining room as Bertie was. But Mr. Caldwell snapped, "You'll finish what's on your plate, boy, do you hear me?"

"Papa, I'm not hungry anymore," said Bertie.

"That's beside the point." Mr. Caldwell shot Ada a simmering glare that seemed to lance right through her. "You'll eat what you're given and be grateful for it."

"That's hardly proper, darling," said Mrs. Caldwell gently.

"I don't care. That child is out of line."

Mrs. Caldwell gave her husband a look so bitterly confused and aching with sorrow that Ada felt a pang of unexpected sympathy for her. She wondered how Mr. Caldwell had been treating her these past two days, ever since Ada had rejected his advance. Mrs. Caldwell looked close to tears. Ada briefly thought of trying to get Mrs. Caldwell on her side; after all, surely, she would be angry with Mr. Caldwell for expressing such bawdy interest in another woman, and Ada had done no wrong. But then again... no. She knew it would be badly received.

So she just kept on doing her duties, with trembling hands and pounding heart, bearing Mr. Caldwell's acid looks and painful jibes anytime she was near him with Bertie. She didn't mind the looks or the harsh words; what she feared was that he might corner her somewhere if she wasn't careful and have his way with her.

Ada took a small breath, trying to calm herself. "Go on, Bertie," she said. "Finish your breakfast."

"I can't imagine why you foolish women insist on calling my son by such a stupid name," barked Mr. Caldwell. "His name is Albert, and you will refer to him as such."

"I'm only Albert when I'm in trouble," said Bertie, regretfully taking another bite.

"Yes, sir," said Ada.

"Darling..." began Mrs. Caldwell.

Before she could say more, the butler came in with a small white envelope in his hand. "A card for you, sir," he said. "The messenger said that it was urgent."

A strange gleam came into Mr. Caldwell's eyes. "Thank you," he said, almost snatching the card from the butler's hand. He seized a letter-opener from beside his plate and eagerly cut through the envelope.

Ada swallowed against her dry mouth. She just wanted to get out of the room, away from Mr. Caldwell.

He held up the card, his eyes sweeping over it, and the corner of his lip curled like the smug snarl of a predator about to pounce. Then he rose to his feet, threw the card down on the table, and pointed at it with an imperious finger.

"I knew it," he cried, his angry shout ringing through the dining room. "Darling, call the police."

Mrs. Caldwell flew to her feet. "What?" she cried. "Why?"

"We have an impostor in our midst," thundered Mr. Caldwell.

Bertie began to cry. Ada scooped him into her arms, partly to calm him, partly to hold him in front of her as a kind of emotional shield. Could it be? Had he found out?

"What on Earth are you talking about?" asked Mrs. Caldwell.

"That girl." Mr. Caldwell pointed straight between Ada's eyes, as though his finger was the barrel of a blunderbuss. "That girl is no governess – in fact, I doubt she's even eighteen years old."

Mrs. Caldwell stared at him. Ada felt as though she'd been drenched with a bucket of ice water; frozen and breathless, she simply gaped.

"This card is from Mrs. Edwards, whose name is on your reference letter, Miss Carter." Mr. Caldwell raised it triumphantly. "Or is that your name at all? Either way, it matters little. Mrs. Edwards has no knowledge of any Ada Carter ever existing. Why, even her niece Bettina doesn't remember anyone by that name."

Ada's stomach clenched. Had Bettina gotten into trouble? Her brief concern was immediately swept aside by the tidal wave of terror washing through her.

"Please, Mr. Caldwell – " she began.

"Is this true?" cried Mrs. Caldwell, turning on her. "Ada, darling – there must be a mistake."

Bertie began to cry harder. "Stop shouting," he sobbed. "Why is everyone shouting?"

"Bertie, darling, please," Ada whispered, bouncing him in her arms.

"Unhand that child," barked Mr. Caldwell. "Fraud and criminal. You have no business in my house. Take your hands off my son."

Mrs. Caldwell rushed across the room, prying Bertie swiftly out of Ada's arms. "Say it's not true," she cried.

Ada opened her mouth, but no sound came out. Her heart burned with agony. Of course, she had been good enough for Mr. Caldwell until she'd rejected him; then he must have found her reference and written to Mrs. Edwards, hoping to find some kind of fuel against her. And what a world of fuel she had given him. There was no coming back from this.

"I'm sorry," she croaked.

"No," gasped Mrs. Caldwell, clutching at Bertie. "Why did you come here? What do you want from us?" Hysteria filled her voice.

"Please, I never hurt anyone," Ada cried. "I was just – I was desperate, and hungry, and – "

"Fraud. Thief," roared Mr. Caldwell. "I should have you arrested. I should call the police."

"I want Miss Ada." Bertie, who so seldom found himself in his own mother's arm, began to kick and scream. "Let me go. Miss Ada. Miss Ada."

His voice became a shrill shriek of fear, and from the head of the table, Ada was appalled by the smug cruelty on the face of Mr. Caldwell as he watched the chaotic scene unfold. This was what happened to girls who rejected him, Ada realized. This was how he felt powerful.

And he was powerful: powerful enough to destroy her life in one fell swoop.

"Take her away," he ordered. "I never want to see her near my family again. And if I do, Miss Carter, I will have you hanged."

The butler was striding toward Ada, who backed away. "Sir, I can explain," she sobbed out.

"Come, Miss Carter," said the butler firmly, grasping her arm.

"Go," roared Mr. Caldwell.

She saw danger in his eyes, saw that the threat he'd made was no idle one. Her thoughts flew to Mama. If she could just keep Mama out of this, then at least her mother would still have work and food and somewhere to stay. She hung her head, her heart hammering, feeling as though the world was tipping under her feet, and allowed the butler to drag her to the door.

Before he exited, however, Mrs. Caldwell cried out. "Is Elsie even your real mother?" she cried.

"Mother?" barked Mr. Caldwell.

Ada swung around, pulling free of the butler. "Please, ma'am, please, say no more," she begged. "Please, she can't go onto the streets. She'll die."

"Answer me," cried Mrs. Caldwell.

"Yes." Ada began to sob. "She is my mother, my poor, poor old mother, and she's going to die if you dismiss her. Please, she's never done anything wrong. Please..."

"Dismiss the mother, too," said Mr. Caldwell furiously.

"Sir," began the butler.

"Do as I say," roared Mr. Caldwell.

A wave of hopeless sobbing gripped Ada, and she could do nothing but allow herself to be dragged away from the life she'd wanted so badly. The life for which she had risked everything.

# CHAPTER 21

JUST YESTERDAY, Ada's savings had seemed like all the money in the world. Even having money to save over the past year had been an unthinkable luxury to her, but since the Caldwells had given her and Mama full board and lodging, there had been little else to spend her money on, apart from some warmer clothes over the winter and a few books that Mama had never read. So she'd squirreled the money away, hoping to find a cottage for Mama someday and to get her out of having to work at all.

But now all those lovely dreams were gone. Now there was just the bleak knowledge that her life's savings were only going to be enough to buy two or three weeks in the run-down boarding house, which smelled like mould, where the walls squeaked of rats and bedbugs, with the threadbare, yellowed curtains hanging over the grimy windows, with the proprietor staring at Ada with little interest.

"Well, do you want the room or not?" he asked angrily.

She had prayed that this room would be affordable. It was better than the other places she'd inquired at, but she'd done the math in her mind instantly: the price for a single person was such that she and Mama would only be able to stay for ten or twelve days before her money ran out. It had taken her two years to become a governess. She knew that searching for work would take far longer than a week or two. Glancing back over her shoulder, she looked through the open front door and into the cold, twilit street. They were running out of time.

"May I see the room?" she asked.

The proprietor sucked at his teeth, then sighed, hoisting his ponderous body from the chair behind the counter. "All right, then," he grumbled. "This way."

Ada knew that he was only helping her at all because of her obviously new and well-made dress; perhaps he hoped that she was some foolish runaway from a well-to-do house, and would soon be found, with a generous reward to the man who had given her somewhere safe to stay. At any rate, she wasn't going to question the faint generosity he was showing her. He led her down a narrow, musty hallway, with cobwebs in the corners and peeling wallpaper, then pushed open a flaking door.

"Here," he grunted. "The lavvy's at the end of the hall."

Ada peered into the room. She ignored the splintering floorboards, the tiny hearth, the straw mattress on the narrow iron bed. Instead, her eyes flew to the window. It was open, allowing in a crisp breath of fresh air from outside. And there was a closet in the corner: not very big, but big enough to squeeze someone inside to hide them.

Someone like Mama.

"Thank you," she said, with all the dignity she could muster. "I'll take the room."

She booked it out for a week, handing the proprietor of the boarding house an appalling amount of her savings. He grumbled off behind the counter again, and Ada excused herself to go shopping, which was only partially true. She and Mama had already bought a little soup for dinner – thin, watery soup that tasted like their days back in the tenement, days to which Ada had promised herself they would never return.

But they were returning. She could feel the tentacles of poverty twining themselves around her arms and legs again, sucking her back like some monster of the deep bent on drowning her.

"Did you get a room?" Mama asked, her eyes hollow. She looked up from where she was sitting on the small trunk that contained everything they owned.

Ada took a deep breath. "Yes, Mama," she said. "And for half the price of the last place, too."

"Half." Mama's eyes brightened a little. "How did you do that?"

"Well…" Ada swallowed. "They don't know that you're here, too. So we'll have to hide you."

"Hide me? How?"

"Don't worry. It's on the ground floor, and there's a big window round the back. You'll just have to pop in through that tonight, and I'll keep you comfortable inside, all right?"

Ada could hear the desperation rising in her voice. Mama studied her hollowly for a few more moments, and Ada found herself wishing once again that Mama would be relieved, or worried, or angry – or anything except dead-eyed like this.

But when she spoke, her voice was utterly toneless. "All right," she said, the uncomplaining sound shattering Ada's heart.

Ada took her mother's hand and led her through the stable yard and around to the back of the boarding house. And as she helped Mama through the window, the indignity of it all was another tentacle. This time it had been thrown around her neck, and it was choking her as it dragged her back into the awful life she thought she'd left behind.

ADA CLENCHED her hands together to hide their shaking as she walked up the familiar sidewalk, keeping her eyes trained on the cracks between the great paving stones. There were sixteen cracks exactly between the street corner and the gate of the Morgan house; she knew because she had skipped over those same cracks many, many times when she was a little girl. Hand-in-hand with Quincy—the only person she could think of who might be able to help her now.

She had just paid the proprietor for another week at the boarding house. No one had discovered Mama yet, and Mama seemed content, or at least indifferent, to stay in the room day in and day out as Ada searched frantically for work. Ada had tried to sound cheerful when she'd told Mama this morning that she was going to try knocking on doors in a different neighbourhood today, trying to see if anyone needed a maid. She knew that her days as a governess were done.

She hadn't told Mama she was going to look for Quincy. She hadn't even told her about the day – just a couple of weeks ago, but it may as well have been a lifetime – when she'd run into Quincy in the park. Mama cried anytime Ada even mentioned the name of Morgan, and she'd long since given up on doing it.

Besides, if telling Mama her plan had given her any hope at all, Ada knew that hope would likely be false. This was what she told her own heart now, as it fluttered at the sight of the tall Morgan house with its familiar silhouette and its spiralling staircases and its glorious, sunny rooms. Quincy had made it very clear at their last meeting that he wasn't willing to help her, even to speak with her for more than two or three minutes.

Except... The way he'd looked at her. The little smile he'd given her, the sincerity in his voice when he'd wished her well. Ada closed her eyes for a moment, relishing the memory. Something had bubbled up in her at that moment, something richly golden that had told her that her feelings for Quincy were far more than just fantasy. And maybe... maybe... Quincy had shared that feeling.

She took a deep breath and strode up the path to the servants' entrance. It was exactly the same as she remembered, except that in Sophia's day, the path had been lined with buttercups and marigolds at this time of year; they had been replaced with staid grey paving stones. Just before she reached the entrance, the door opened and none other than Macy stepped out.

Ada startled, only just stopping herself from calling out the erstwhile scullery-maid's name. Macy was taller than Ada now, and she wore a very neat uniform; the dress of a parlourmaid. Ada felt a rush of relief and regret at the sight of the girl. She realized, now, why poor Macy had always disliked her, and at the same time felt a pang of jealousy. If only she could have stayed in the Morgan house all this time.

"Hello," she croaked out.

Macy looked up. There was no recognition in her eyes; they flashed over Ada's expensive dress, and she gave a confused little curtsy. "May I help you, my lady?"

Ada considered, briefly, telling Macy who she was. But no. The girl would never help her then.

"I'm sorry to trouble you, but I'm looking for Master Quincy Morgan," she said.

Macy stared at her. "You've just missed him. He rode down the street just two minutes ago."

"When do you think he'll be back?" Ada asked, swallowing her nervousness.

Macy shook her head. "I don't think you understand," she said. "He won't be back at all. He's left the house."

"Left the house." The thought was incomprehensible. "But why?"

"I don't know, ma'am. They don't tell me these things."

Ada's heart pounded in her ears. She had to find Quincy before he disappeared from her life forever.

"Which way did he go?" she asked breathlessly.

Macy pointed, and Ada spun around and ran down the drive, turning down the street, bolting pell-mell down the sidewalk, desperate to cling to what felt like her last hope.

❈

SOMEHOW, by a brilliant stroke of luck, she caught up to him.

Her heart was racing, her lungs burning when Ada ran around the bend in the street, her dress soaked with sweat from the running. At first, she saw nothing; it was a Saturday afternoon, and not a thing stirred on the street. Her heart faltered in her. He was gone, and she would never see him again, and now all that was left for her was the wharves...

Then she saw it: the flash of a chestnut hide. Her feet stuttered on the pavement, and she jogged a little faster, and Quincy's chestnut horse came into view. It was standing on three legs on the pavement, trembling, and Quincy was bent over one of its hooves, using a hoof-pick to dig a stone out between the foot and the shoe.

Ada was so breathless and so tearful with relief that for a few seconds she could only blunder to a halt and stand there, her chest heaving with effort, and sweat trickling down the sides of her face. Quincy was absorbed in prying out the stone and didn't look up until she spoke.

"Quincy," she breathed.

He jumped, looking up, fear flashing briefly across her face. It was replaced at once with joy.

"Ada." He set down the horse's foot and strode toward her, holding out his arms. "Oh, I'm so glad to see you."

"You are?" Ada panted.

Quincy grasped her hands in his own, squeezing them gently. "Of course, I am. I've been searching for you everywhere."

Ada stared up at him, silent and unbelieving.

"I thought you said you worked for the Caldwells," he said.

"I did," said Ada. "I – I was dismissed."

"No one would tell me anything, so I went on searching…" Quincy stopped, his eyes alight. "But it doesn't matter now. You're here now."

"Why were you looking for me?" Ada whispered. "I thought… I thought you wanted nothing to do with me."

A dark flush of shame crept over Quincy's cheeks. He hung his head. "I should never have ridden away from you the way I did," he said quietly. "I was a coward. I have been a coward ever since you and Elsie and Mama were taken away from me, Ada. I was alone except for my father, and so I did everything I could to please him. But I never could. I never did. And when I saw you, and I saw how pleased you were to see me, and I realized that I've been chasing approval from a man who never loved me, when… when… when there were other people in my life who did love me."

Ada stared into his eyes, her heart fluttering. Had Quincy been about to say something else, something he feared might sound too forward?

"Papa has been beastly," said Quincy. "He beat me when I was a child and manipulates me now, and seeing you made me realize that the business and the inheritance were never worth it. I... I stood up to him at last."

"Oh, Quincy," Ada cried, with a rush of spontaneous joy.

"I suppose I love my father in a way, but he's cruel and what he did to you and your mama was so, so wrong. He was cruel to my mother, too, and he's never changed. He never will," Quincy added bitterly. "He threw me out of the house, and I wasn't even sorry."

"Threw you out?" Ada stared at him, pride and worry mingling in her chest. Her own struggles seemed to have fallen by the wayside in her joy to see him. "Where will you go?"

"Oh, don't worry about me." Quincy laughed. "I'm just riding across town to my uncle's house. He married my papa's sister, and she's been gone for a while, but Uncle Ralph and I have always stayed friends."

*Ralph.* The name sent a chilling memory sliding down Ada's spine. She remembered being hidden away anytime Master Ralph had come to the Morgan house, but judging from the gleam in Quincy's eye, he still enjoyed his uncle's visits.

"I'm glad you're all right," she said, relieved.

"I'm just fine. Don't worry about me," said Quincy. "Now – tell me what happened to you. Are you all right? Where are you staying? Do you have work again?"

Shame welled up in Ada's heart, yet somehow, she still found herself telling Quincy the full story. Somehow, she still felt that she could trust him with all her heart, despite the many years that had passed since she had been thrown out of the Morgan house. And she was right. When she concluded the sorry tale, there was no judgment in Quincy's eyes.

"Ada, I'm so sorry," he said, squeezing her hands again. "But you don't need to worry. I left Papa's house so that I could find you and your mother... the only people alive who ever truly cared for me. And I'm going to help you both, I promise." He smiled. "Uncle Ralph will have a position for you, I'm sure – perhaps as a scribe or something. He's always helping girls with work, and since you're a friend of mine, he'll be happy to help."

"Oh, he will? Do you think so?" Ada asked, her hopes leaping wildly in her chest.

"Of course, I do. And Elsie, too – I'm sure of it. You don't need to be afraid. In fact, I'll speak to him tonight, and then you can bring your mother to his house tomorrow morning."

"Quincy..." Ada's eyes filled with tears.

"Please don't cry," Quincy pleaded. "Everything will be all right." He opened a saddlebag and rummaged in it, extricating a card. "Here is Uncle Ralph's address, and here is enough money for a cab to take you back to the house where you're staying and then to drive you to Uncle Ralph's house in the morning."

Ada stared down at the card, her heart pounding with relief. "I don't know what to say, Quincy."

"You don't have to say anything." He smiled at her, and he was the way he had always been as a boy, with shining eyes and a mischievous grin. "Just come. I want you and Elsie back... I hope you can forgive me for the way I stood by when Papa dismissed you."

"You were just a boy. Of course, we forgive you," said Ada.

Tears welled up in Quincy's eyes. "Thank you, Ada. Thank you," he said. "Will you be safe in a cab going back to the boarding house? Should I go with you?"

"No, no. It's all right. Take your horse to your uncle's house and talk to him about us... and we'll see you in the morning." Ada laughed with the sheer wonder of those words.

Quincy beamed, his smile both sincere and tearful. "I can't wait to see you. Are you sure you'll be all right?"

Ada let out a long sigh of relief.

"Yes," she said, with conviction. "Yes, thank you, Quincy. We'll be just fine now."

# CHAPTER 22

ADA WAS SO excited when she burst through the door of her room that she almost called out loudly to her mother. She only just managed to muffle her happy cry so that no one else would notice that she'd smuggled Mama inside.

"Mama," she hissed in a delighted whisper. "Mama, you'll never guess what happened."

Mama looked up from where she was sitting on the edge of the bed, staring at the floor. There was no hope in her eyes as she looked up at Ada. "What is it?" she asked, with no emotion.

"I saw Quincy." Ada fell to her knees in front of her mother, taking her hands. "I saw Quincy, and he's going to help us."

"He is?" Mama's eyes widened, a spark of life flickering in them. "How? What about Simon?"

"He's not staying with Master Simon anymore. He realized that Master Simon has only ever been cruel to him, so he left."

"He left." Mama gave a small smile. "Oh, I'm glad. I've always felt sorry for that poor child with his dreadful father."

Already, life was coming back into her mother. Ada beamed, squeezing Mama's hands. "Now he's going to live with his uncle, and we're going to go there too. He's going to give us work there. Everything is going to be all right – he even gave me some money for the cab to go there tomorrow morning."

Suddenly, Mama's face froze. She pulled her hands away. "His uncle?" she said slowly.

"Yes," said Ada. "Master Ralph. Do you remember him?"

Mama looked away, her face frozen with something that could have been fear. "Yes," she whispered huskily. "I remember him." A slow, glittering tear rolled down her cheek.

"Mama, what on Earth is wrong?" asked Ada, thoroughly alarmed. Mama hadn't cried at all since they'd left the Morgan house.

Mama took a few long, shaky breaths. Then she turned to look at Ada, and her eyes were cold and hard.

"We can never go to Ralph Warden's house, Ada," she said, her voice glittering with brittle rage. "Never. Do you understand? He can never see you – or me – ever again."

Ada stared at Mama, uncomprehending. "What are you talking about?" she cried. "Mama, this is our only chance."

Mama stood up from the bed, giving Ada a terrifying stare.

"No," she said, her voice rising. "I won't have you within a hundred feet of him, Ada. Never."

"Mama, hush," Ada cried, alarmed. "Someone will find you."

"I don't care, Ada." Mama's voice rose to a sharp pitch. "I don't care about anything other than keeping you away from that monster."

"Monster?" Ada gasped. "What are you talking about?"

Mama stopped, breathing hard, staring at Ada, her body trembling.

Ada swallowed, a memory coming back to her. "One time when Ralph visited the Morgans, you and Sophia were talking outside my door," she said slowly. "You said... you said you'd tell me when I was older."

"I suppose you're older." Mama sank down onto the bed again, as though her outburst had sapped all of her strength. "I'd hoped you would never need to find out, Ada. But I suppose you have to understand why you can never go near him."

Ada sat down slowly beside her mother. "What happened?" she asked softly.

Mama dashed at a tear that was threatening to roll down her cheek.

"I was only seventeen," she said quietly. "I'd just been hired as a lady's maid for my dear Sophia." Her voice cracked. "I grew up in poverty and becoming a lady's maid was the most important thing in the world to me. I loved working for Sophia; even from the beginning, she was always kind to me. Kinder than most people would be." She paused. "That was when I met Ralph – just two months after I'd started working as Sophia's maid."

Ada waited and sensing danger in the story, her stomach curled at the thought.

"He was so dashing. So handsome." Mama's voice turned bitter. "He visited for a week, and he kept talking to me every time he caught me alone, and he caught me alone more and more often. I thought he was kind. I thought he was lovely... until he... he made an advance on me."

Ada thought of Mr. Caldwell, and her stomach knotted. "Was he angry when you rejected him?"

"Of course, he was." Mama wasn't looking at her. "Angry enough that he threw me to the ground and had his way with me in the study when no one else was home to hear me scream."

Ada squeezed her eyes tightly shut, the abomination of it all stinging her belly like nausea. "Mama…"

"He said he would never tell if I didn't," said Mama, rushing on as though to avoid that terrible part of the story. "So I didn't. Being Sophia's maid was all I had. I couldn't lose that. When I realized I was pregnant, I thought that was the end of it. I told Sophia I'd been accosted, but not who accosted me – not until much later, of course, when you were bigger. She kept me on. No other lady would ever have done it, but she did." Mama was crying now. "She was special."

Ada put an arm around Mama's shoulders, feeling her own body tremble with the shock. "So… Quincy's uncle Ralph is my father?"

"Yes," Mama whispered.

Ada felt, at first, a twist of revulsion in the pit of her belly at the thought that she was the product of such an unspeakable act. Then, a rush of horror, followed by relief. Ralph was Quincy's uncle, but he was no blood relative. That meant that she and Quincy were not relatives, either.

So they could be…

Could be *what?* Her stomach plummeted at the memory of Quincy's face, his excitement as he told her that he was going to live with Ralph. He was so happy. Happy to be free of his father, and certain that Ralph would take care of him. But Ada knew that if she told Quincy the truth, he would never see his uncle in the same way again. He would never be able to stay with his uncle.

Tears trickled down her cheeks. She had to keep the truth from Quincy, or he would abandon the last hope he had, and become as destitute as she and Mama were. She couldn't wish that fate on anyone, least of all the boy she'd always cared for... who had become the man she loved.

"Promise me you won't go near Ralph," Mama pushed. "Promise me, Ada."

"I promise," Ada croaked.

Mama sagged back onto the bed, pale and exhausted by her high emotion. Ada took a few deep breaths and put on the kettle to make her mother some tea.

She was out of options. But one thing was certain: she wouldn't drag Quincy into the same position that she was.

# CHAPTER 23

ADA'S HEART THROBBED, the same steady ache that had kept her awake all night. Her sorrow and exhaustion seemed to have filled her veins with lead; her feet weighed tons apiece, and she had to drag them as she slopped up the street, the great anchor dragging once again at her shoulders.

She knew she should be happy as she trudged up the street toward the boarding house. She should be pleased she had found a job on the wharf, even if it was just picking oakum, even if it would leave her with squinting eyes and gnarled hands, even if she would make only a tiny pittance, not enough for both food and lodging, not enough that Mama could rest. Even if she would have to take her mother down to the wharf tomorrow and find her a similarly back-breaking, menial job with a similarly cruel, heartless boss.

At least it was something. And something was better than nothing, especially at a time like this, when Ada once again teetered over the abyss of having nothing at all.

She tried not to think of her father. She tried not to think of Bertie. Above all, she tried not to think of Quincy.

But it was impossible, because he was waiting for her at the door of the boarding house, his fine chestnut horse a spot of pure splendour under the feeble, guttering light of the grubby streetlamp. He looked tired and rumpled, sitting in a heap at the front door, his hat by his side, his hair sticking out in all directions.

Ada felt a surge of guilt. She'd imagined he would forget her and carry on with his life when she failed to show up this morning, but his filthy boots and his pale face spoke of a long day spent searching.

He looked up when her footsteps sounded in the street, and struggled at once to his feet, his eyes wide. "Ada," he gasped. "There you are. I was so afraid..." He stopped, seeing the look on her face. "Are you all right?"

Looking into his big blue eyes, Ada realized that this would be the hardest thing she had ever done in her life. But it needed to be done. She had to hurt him, and she knew that she would never be able to do it except to save him. And saving him was everything.

She dug in her pocket, pulling out the money he'd given her for the cab.

"I'm sorry I didn't bring this back earlier," she said. "It's yours." She held it out.

He stared at it, then back at her. "What are you doing?" he asked. "It's for you. You were meant to bring a cab to Uncle Ralph's house this morning. Don't you remember?" Confusion and worry mingled on his face.

Ada took a deep breath. The only way to do this was suddenly and sharply, or she would never manage.

"We're not coming," she said. "I'm sorry."

"Not... coming?" Quincy stared at her as though this was incomprehensible.

"I'm sorry," Ada repeated. "We can't come." She pushed past him, going toward the door.

"Ada." Quincy grasped her arm in a gentle, trembling hand. "What's happening? Please... tell me why." His eyes filled with tears. "How have I wronged you?"

"Oh, Quincy." Ada swallowed her own tears, her voice softening. "You have never wronged me. It's nothing you did."

"Then why...?"

"I can't tell you. We just can't come." She pulled her arm away gently, laid a hand on his chest. She could feel the thudding of his heart through her trembling palm. "I want you to go away."

He reeled back as though she'd struck him.

"Go away?" he breathed huskily. "Ada... you and Elsie are the only people left alive who've ever really loved me." He sniffed. "Except Ralph, perhaps."

"Ralph does love you," said Ada, willing it to be true. "You're going to be all right with him. I want you to go now, Quincy. Take your horse and ride back to Ralph and live the beautiful life that you deserve." She turned away so that he wouldn't see her crying.

"Ada, please." Quincy's voice broke. "I want to help you."

"I know you do. But you can't." Ada hated the harshness in her tone. "Please go."

She laid her hand on the doorknob, and Quincy's voice came to her, shattered to pieces, filled with a love she'd only ever dreamed of and now had to walk away from.

"I'll go if you want me to," he said shakily. "I'll do as you wish, Ada, but I need you... I need you to know that I love you." His voice wavered, but his conviction never did. "I'll always be ready to help you if you need it."

Ada's tears streaked down her face. She wanted to respond – to say what? The truth, that she loved him, too? But she had to make him leave for his own good, and she could utter not a single word through the throbbing lump in her throat. So she just went inside, and closed the door quietly behind her: closed it on Quincy, and on her last bit of hope.

ADA'S HANDS CRAMPED CONSTANTLY, and she was only five hours into a shift that lasted for twelve.

She ignored the pain and her broken nails and torn cuticles and the steady sting of agony on her back as she sat huddled on a narrow wooden stool, bent over a length of rope that lay on the floor in front of her. It was thicker than her arm; coarse, heavy stuff that had already thrust a thousand tiny bristles into her fingertips, making them sting with each movement. On her left side there lay a little heap of fibres – bits of untwisted rope that she'd painfully torn off the big rope in her hands. It was old and frayed, but the centre still seemed to be impossibly strong.

She picked up the rusty nail lying on a workbench beside her and applied it fervently to the middle of the rope, trying to pry a few more fibres loose. Some of them came away; then the nail slipped, digging painfully into her palm.

"Ouch," Ada whispered to herself.

She felt eyes on her and looked to her right. Mama sat beside her, silent, her eyes empty where they brushed over Ada. Seeing no blood, Mama turned back to the rope that lay in front of her and started to pick at it. Her own hands were scratched and bleeding. The heap of fibres beside her was even smaller than Ada's.

Quietly, Ada picked up a handful of her fibres and put them down on top of Mama's to make Mama's pile bigger. That way the boss's rage would be deflected onto Ada. Mama appeared not to notice. Mama didn't notice anything anymore. It was as though her outburst about Ralph three days ago had drained her of the last of her spirit.

Everything ached within Ada. She was sitting right beside her mother, yet she had never been so alone. Her mind kept wandering back to the thing she had subconsciously regarded as her final hope for all of her life: Quincy. She couldn't stop hearing his words outside the boarding house last night.

*I love you.*

And he had shown her that he did, by doing something that no man in her life had ever done: respecting her choice. She wondered how much time he'd spent combing through boarding houses in the area, asking for a girl named Ada Carter. How long he'd waited on the doorstep in that reeking, filthy part of London. Only to walk away when she had asked him to.

A tear slid down her cheek, and she brushed it away quickly to keep it from falling onto the rope. He was everything she'd ever dreamed of.

And she had let him go.

Another gust of rain blew in under the little overhang where she and Mama were sitting, bringing with it the steady stench of the Thames that rolled by at the edge of the wharf just a few feet away. Ada shivered slightly, then started picking at the rope with more vigour. It would warm her up even if it tore her hands to shreds.

Her mind felt empty, deserted by anything of interest. She reached for a few numbers, hoping to keep it occupied. *Divide seventy-three by four, to two decimal points.* She fumbled for the answer, but it was gone. What was the point? She had railed against her fate, fought it, even thought she'd been victorious. But she wasn't.

This was all that was left now: the struggle. And when she glanced over at Mama, saw her hands fumbling with the rope, the paleness in her face, heard the rattle in her breathing, she knew there was not much struggle left for Mama anymore. Her life would soon be over, and perhaps that would be a mercy somehow.

The day dragged on. It rained; a puddle formed at their feet, and Ada moved the oakum fibres out of the way. Her feet grew wetter and wetter. An ominous tickle began at the back of her nose. Mama began to cough. Gaggles of sailors passed them by from time to time, barking out cat-calls, wolf whistling. Now that Ada knew Mama's history, each lewd glance sent a jagged knife through her soul. They had a brief break at one o' clock for a crust of bread and a cup of water, and then they went on, Ada's hands cramping, Mama moving more and more slowly, Ada scrambling to pick enough fibres for the both of them.

Their boss, a shipwright, was still not happy. When Mama and Ada brought their bundles of fibres to him where he was mixing tar for caulking, he gave them a long, blank look.

"Where's the rest?" he demanded.

Ada took a deep breath. "That's all there is, sir," she said. "It's my fault. I hurt my hand with the nail, and it made me slow."

He gave the blue puncture in her palm a dissatisfied look. "Well, I can't give you sixpence each for this," he said in disgust. "You'll have sixpence and thruppence and not a farthing more."

Ada's heart faltered. Nine pennies. It was even more of a pittance than usual. "Sir..." she began.

"Are you arguing?" asked the shipwright, looking up from his tar and studying her with angry, beady eyes.

Ada took a deep breath.

"No," she mumbled.

He dug in a pocket, producing the two small coins, and dropped them into Ada's palm. "Don't be late tomorrow," he barked.

Ada nodded, took Mama's hand, and led her away. Her mind grappled with the dreadful mathematics of their situation. Food, or rent? Food, or rent? How could she make that choice? Rain drove against her face, and Mama coughed.

They had just passed the shipwright's shop and were heading down the alley leading into the street toward home when Ada felt it. A presence, somewhere in front of them; a change in the slip of streetlight that shone into the alley. She stopped, her heart suddenly hammering in her chest.

"Ada, let's go home," Mama croaked. She was shivering, her eyes red; Ada was sure she had a fever.

"Do you see someone, over there?" Ada asked, pointing.

A shadow unfolded itself from the darkness, rising against the light, the silhouette of a tall man in a long coat, his ponytail hanging neatly on his shoulders. It was a silhouette Ada had seen many times as she peered through keyholes and cracks in curtains to watch Quincy playing with his uncle.

It was Ralph.

Ada could feel simmering hostility radiating from the man's figure in waves even before he opened his mouth and spoke in a malicious hiss.

"Hello, daughter."

Mama stiffened beside her. Ada grabbed her arm, spinning her around.

"Run, Mama," she shouted. "Back to the shipwright. Run."

Somehow her cry spurred life back into Mama, and she bolted, heading for the office, and Ada whirled around, her hands clenched into fists, her teeth gritted. She knew that this tall man would catch up to Mama in seconds, throw her to the ground, hurt her again the way he had hurt her seventeen years ago – unless she stopped him. And even as he sidled nearer, Ada was ready to stop him. She would fight him fist and foot, tooth and nail if she had to. She expected to feel fear, and it was there, simmering somewhere inside her; but there was a raging fire in her chest, and she leaned into that burning rage.

"I know what you did to my mother," she snarled.

"She was beautiful, your mother," said Ralph. He took a step nearer; streetlight fell over his face, the cold features, the dark eyes that travelled around her body in a nauseating manner. "Like you."

"How did you find us?" Ada demanded. "What have you done to Quincy?" Fear quivered in her gut.

"Nothing at all," said Ralph. "The dear boy is at home, moping over you, of course. When he told me that the girl who'd broken his heart was Ada Carter, I knew why you'd rejected the offer of staying here."

Ada felt a faint pang of relief. Quincy was all right, and Mama must be safe now. She started to back away, planning to flee.

"You're a monster," she said, her words floating through the air with conviction.

He blinked. "What?"

Ada felt a sudden, heady tide of something that could have been courage or simply drunken adrenaline. She realized that no one had ever stood up to this man before. No one had ever told him to his face that what he did was wrong.

"You're a monster," she repeated. "Preying on innocent women – *girls*." She realized that Mama had only been the age she was now when Ralph had accosted her. "You're a disgrace."

A dangerous gleam came into his eye, and he took a step toward her. "Watch your tongue, wench," he spat.

"I hope you feel shame," said Ada. "I hope you realize that you're disgusting, and that you never hurt anyone ever again."

Ralph let out a wordless roar, throwing himself toward her. Ada leaped back, ready to flee – and her foot found an empty tin, which spun away underneath her, and she fell on her back, stars popping in front of her eyes, and he was upon her. Huge hands smashed down onto her shoulders, pinning her to the earth; she screamed, thrashed with her legs, but he rammed a knee down painfully on her thighs and she was trapped, trapped, trapped, his hands creeping toward her neck, taking a stranglehold.

"Let me go." Ada screamed as his fingers began to squeeze her throat. "Help. *Help!*"

"No one's coming," hissed Ralph, with a terrifying chuckle. "No one comes for girls like you."

Ada sucked down a breath and tried to scream again, but his hands tightened around her throat, and the breath wouldn't go out. She managed a trembling wheeze, tried to breathe in, but nothing was coming in or out.

"It's a pity, I know," Ralph hissed. "But I can't let anyone else find out about your mother and me, now that she's blabbing. The scandal would ruin me."

She was thrashing but her limbs lashed blindly; she was staring into Ralph's face, but his cruel grimace was fading in front of her eyes. She was... losing feeling... her hands and feet... disappearing. She tried again... her chest moved... nothing came... there was pain... fading... fading...

Then a scream. "Leave her alone!"

The hands loosened on her neck, and Ada drew a long, shaking, painful breath. He was still kneeling on her; the breath seemed to bring back a world of pain, and she felt herself fading again when another cry brought her back.

"What are you doing? Let her go."

It was Quincy – dear, dear Quincy – here in her hour of need. His voice was brilliant sunshine piercing the darkness in her soul. "Quincy, help," she shrieked.

Ralph slapped her. The blow was unexpected, blood bursting into her mouth, and it spurred an animal sound from Quincy, something rage-filled and deafening, a lion's roar. She heard slapping footsteps, a yelp of surprise from Ralph, and then Quincy slammed into him, and they both fell backwards into the dark alley. There was a meaty thud, fist meeting bone.

"Quincy," Ada shrieked, scrambling to her feet. "Quincy."

The struggling men rolled into the light of the streetlamp, and there was blood in Quincy's hair; he had gripped both of Ralph's wrists, struggling to keep them away from his face, and Ralph was writhing and struggling and screaming.

"Just stop, uncle." Quincy shouted. "Just stop."

But Ralph wasn't going to stop. His eyes were wild now, manic, and Ada knew that Quincy was in more danger than he thought. Her eyes lit on a piece of plank leaning against the alley wall. As the men rolled closer to her, she grabbed the plank, raising it in one hand, her blood pounding. Just then, Ralph ripped his right wrist free of Quincy's grip.

"You've made a terrible mistake interfering in this, boy," he growled, pulled back his fist, ready to strike a blow that could kill Quincy –

Ada swung the plank. It thudded into the back of Ralph's head, and he fell forward onto his face, and lay groaning in the gutter.

"Ada!" Quincy scrambled to his feet and rushed to her, throwing his arms around her and hugging her close to his trembling body. "Oh, Ada, Ada, are you all right?"

"I-I'm fine," Ada said, her voice rasping hoarsely from the half-strangling. "Oh – Quincy, you're bleeding."

He stepped back, a trickle of blood running down his cheek from his temple. "It's all right. It's nothing," he said.

Ada dabbed at it with her sleeve. "I thought he was going to kill you," she whispered.

"He was going to kill *you*. I saw it in his eyes." A terrible shudder ran down Quincy's spine. "But... but why?"

Ada squeezed Quincy's hand.

"Is that what you couldn't tell me?" Quincy asked softly.

"Yes," said Ada. "You'd never see your uncle the same way again. You wouldn't go with him." Tears flooded her eyes. "And Quincy, your life would be ruined."

"I don't care," said Quincy fiercely. "I can't believe my sweet uncle nearly killed you, Ada. He's nothing to me anymore," he added with disgust. "Tell me what he did."

Ada paused, but she knew there was no reason to hide it anymore. She told him gently, and he grew very pale and sank down onto a broken old pallet lying under the streetlamp.

"I wouldn't believe it unless I'd just seen that," he quavered.

"I'm sorry," said Ada softly. Her tears spilled over. "Quincy, I'm so sorry. What will you do now? He... he's going to wake up... I..."

"I'm going to hand him over to the police," said Quincy grimly.

"But what about you? You'll be ruined."

"No... no, I won't." Quincy slumped for a moment, suddenly looking young and overwhelmed with his dishevelled hair hanging in a quiff over his forehead.

"What do you mean?"

"That's what I came down here to tell you. The man at the boarding house said you were at work at the wharves, and when I came down here..." Quincy shook his head at the horror of the scene he'd encountered. "Ada ... my father's dead."

The words tolled through her like a death knell.

"D-dead?" she stammered.

"Yes. A heart attack. His lawyer called on me this afternoon." Quincy stared up at her. "I wish we hadn't parted as harshly as we did." Tears quivered in his eyes.

"Oh... Quincy." Ada's heart stung for him. Somehow, he'd lost his father and his uncle in a single day. "I'm so sorry."

"I think h-he was sorry, too." Quincy wiped at his eyes. "Because he hadn't changed his will. I've inherited every-thing." He looked up at her. "Morgan House is mine."

Ada stared at him, but she could not utter a single word.

"I'm sorry about my father, but I'm glad of one thing." Quincy reached out, gripping both of her hands in his. "I have some-where to take you now, Ada. Somewhere safe. A home." His tears spilled over. "If you'll come. And your mother. Please, please... say that you'll come."

It was all so much. Terror, hope, relief, exhaustion, pain, grief, courage, joy – it washed over Ada in waves upon waves, washing away everything, the passage of the years, the over-whelming chaos of the day, leaving only one monument standing among the crashing waters of her emotions: love. Unbearable love.

"Please take us home," she whispered.

Then she fell into his arms, and as he held her, they both wept. But this time, they wept together.

# EPILOGUE

*FIVE YEARS Later*

ANOTHER WAVE of agony wracked Ada's body, and she let out a long, rising scream as her body curled with pain. Her finger-nails dug into the soft flesh of the back of her knees where she gripped them; her scream grew hoarse, and the pain passed, and she fell back onto the sweaty pillows, gasping for breath.

"Almost," cried the midwife. "You're doing wonderfully, ma'am. One more good push."

"Mama," Ada croaked. "Mama."

Mama had not let go of her hand since her water had broken. She squeezed it now, her eyes full of a fierce and blazing love that took Ada's breath away.

"You're nearly there, darling," she said. "Nearly there. In a moment, you'll hold your baby. Just one more push."

The thought of holding her child filled Ada with a ferocious determination. She sat up, gritted her teeth, and leaned into the next contraction, letting out a roar as she pushed with all her might and fell back once again.

"Yes. Yes," cried the midwife.

The pain receded, and Ada had time only for a brief pang of worry before the baby's cries filled the air.

"It's a little girl. A perfect little girl," cried the midwife, ecstatic.

Ada struggled to sit up. "I want her," she gasped, sweat trickling down her back. "Please give her to me."

Mama had already swaddled the baby in a blanket, and she held it out to Ada. Somehow, Ada's entire world condensed down into that little scrunched-up face, the toothless mouth howling, the little fists waving above the tiny head. The baby was dirty and blotchy and the most beautiful thing she had ever seen in her life. She clutched the baby close to her, tears streaming inexplicably down her cheeks even though this was the happiest moment of her existence.

"Oh – oh," she breathed, sobbing with joy. "Oh, hello, darling."

The baby's cries began to calm, and as Mama and the midwife fussed around taking away the dirty linen and covering Ada, she opened her little eyes. They were the bluest of blues, just like her father's.

"Oh, my sweet baby," Ada whispered.

Mama sat on the edge of the bed beside her. "She looks exactly like her father did, when he was born," she said softly. When she looked up at Ada, her smile filled the world. "He was born right here in this very room. You were lying on that couch, nothing more than a baby yourself."

"Mama, thank you," Ada sobbed out, joy swamping her. "Thank you." She swallowed. "Please – can Quincy come in and see her?"

"Of course," said the midwife. "You're both ready."

She opened the door, and Quincy burst in, his tie and hair in disarray, his blue eyes very wide, so much like his daughter's.

"Ada," he cried, rushing to her.

"It's a girl," Ada gasped. "It's a little girl."

She saw his entire world change as he stared down at the baby, one arm cuddled closely around her shoulders.

"She's so perfect," he gasped.

"Of course, she is." Ada leaned against him. "She's your daughter."

"Have you chosen a name for her yet?" Mama asked softly.

Ada and Quincy exchanged a glance, and Quincy turned to Mama, putting a hand on her shoulder.

"Sophia," he said. "Her name is Sophia. Sophie, for short."

Mama's eyes spilled over with happy tears.

"I love you all so much," she said.

She wrapped her arms around Quincy, and then they were all enfolded in one great embrace with baby Sophie in the middle. The baby gurgled, gazing up at the world with huge, uncomprehending eyes. She would never know the hardships her mother and father had known. There would be no abusive father, no dreadful past, no endless work, no cruelty.

And no poverty. Once and for all, Ada and her mother were free from its dread clutches.

She raised the baby to her face and kissed her again and again, then whispered a promise to the new-born girl.

"We all will love you and watch out for you as long as you live."


The End

# CONTINUE READING...

THANK you for reading **The Fraudulent Governess! Are you wondering what to read next?** Why not read **The Forgotten Widow's Christmas? Here's a sneak peek for you:**

Tilly was breathless with laughter, bent double as she chased after her toddler. Lissa's chubby legs were pumping, her brown curls streaming over her shoulders as she ran, squealing with delight. Her little knitted hat had blown off somewhere in their mad game of tag, but despite the snow crunching under Tilly's feet, she felt a flush of warmth on her cheeks.

"I'm going to get you," she sang out, stretching out her arms toward Lissa.

"No, no," Lissa giggled, dodging left and right. "I'll escape."

"Oh, Lissa, you're so fast." Tilly laughed, carefully measuring her steps to stay a few feet behind the little girl. "I'll never catch you."

Lissa glanced over her shoulder, her cheeks very pink, her eyes as blue as the wintry sky above their heads. They danced with excitement, but glancing back was her mistake. Her tiny shoe caught on a tree root, and she fell headlong and face-first into the snow.

Tilly skidded to a halt, quick to prevent the howling tantrum that might ensue. "Oh, Lissa, look at you," she giggled. "You're playing tag, not making snow angels, you silly girl."

Her light tone worked. Unhurt, Lissa rolled onto her back, snowflakes like stars in her dark hair, eyes shining. "Snow angels," she chuckled, and started waving her arms and legs vigorously in the soft, white powder.

"Snow angels," Tilly announced dramatically, falling onto her back beside Lissa and getting started on one of her own.

"I'm going to make the biggest one," roared four-year-old Robby, throwing himself down beside his mother and waving his limbs madly.

"You're all so silly." Janie, the eldest at six, stomped over to them with her little hands on her hips and a look of great disdain on her long, solemn face. "You can't just change the game right in the middle of playing it."

"Yes, I can," said Lissa, sitting up abruptly. She seized a fistful of snow and flung it at Janie. "Snowball fight!"

The snow hit Janie squarely in the face, and she gasped at the cold. Annoyance flashed over her small features for a second, melting away when she saw Lissa's happy face. "Oh, you're going to be sorry you started it." She giggled, grabbing a handful of snow, and moulding it quickly into a ball.

Utter chaos ensued. Snowballs were flying everywhere; Lissa was running for cover behind the oak tree, Tilly was dithering and wondering which side to join, and Robby was joyously continuing with his snow angel, oblivious to the madness around him. It was several minutes before the children calmed down and they all fell on a heap on the wooden bench under the old oak tree whose great, gnarled limbs stretched over the postage stamp of garden behind their tiny cottage.

Tilly wrapped her arms around the children, hugging them all close. She wondered how long it would be before they were too big to all fit into her arms at once. Although she knew she should be excited for that day – the day when they could start to earn their own keep – her heart longed for days like these to last forever. What could be more perfect than playing with her children on a winter's day like this? And it was a perfect winter's day, with the balmy sunshine making all the snow sparkle, and the cold breeze keeping it all frozen in picturesque, glimmering white.

## **Click Here to Continue Reading!**

https://www.ticahousepublishing.com/victorian-romance.html

# THANKS FOR READING

IF YOU LOVE VICTORIAN ROMANCE, **Click Here**

https://victorian.subscribemenow.com/

to hear about all **New Faye Godwin Romance Releases! I will let you know as soon as they become available!**

Thank you, Friends! If you enjoyed *The Fraudulent Governess,* would you kindly take a couple minutes to leave a positive review on Amazon? It only takes a moment, and positive reviews truly make a difference. Thank you so much! I appreciate it!

Much love,

Faye Godwin

# MORE FAYE GODWIN
## VICTORIAN ROMANCES!

**We love rich, dramatic Victorian Romances and have a library of Faye Godwin titles just for you!** (Remember that ALL of Faye's Victorian titles can be downloaded FREE with Kindle Unlimited!)

**CLICK HERE to discover Faye's Complete Collection of Victorian Romance!**

https://ticahousepublishing.com/victorian-romance.html

# ABOUT THE AUTHOR

Faye Godwin has been fascinated with Victorian Romance since she was a teen. After reading every Victorian Romance in her public library, she decided to start writing them herself —which she's been doing ever since. Faye lives with her husband and young son in England. She loves to travel throughout her country, dreaming up new plots for her romances. She's delighted to join the Tica House Publishing family and looks forward to getting to know her readers.

contact@ticahousepublishing.com

Printed in Great Britain
by Amazon

82574381R00153